alpaca
my
bags

alpaca my bags

Jenny Goebel

Scholastic Inc.

Copyright © 2020 by Jenny Goebel

All rights reserved. Published by Scholastic Inc., *Publishers since 1920*. SCHOLASTIC and associated logos are trademarks and/or registered trademarks of Scholastic Inc.

The publisher does not have any control over and does not assume any responsibility for author or third-party websites or their content.

No part of this publication may be reproduced, stored in a retrieval system, or transmitted in any form or by any means, electronic, mechanical, photocopying, recording, or otherwise, without written permission of the publisher. For information regarding permission, write to Scholastic Inc., Attention: Permissions Department, 557 Broadway, New York, NY 10012.

This book is a work of fiction. Names, characters, places, and incidents are either the product of the author's imagination or are used fictitiously, and any resemblance to actual persons, living or dead, business establishments, events, or locales is entirely coincidental.

ISBN 978-1-338-60890-8

10 9 8 7 6 5 4 3 2 1   20 21 22 23 24

Printed in the U.S.A.   40

First printing 2020

Book design by Yaffa Jaskoll

For the family and friends who keep me rooted.
And for my adventurous crew,
Matt, Ethan, Logan, and Lucas—
I'll pack my bags for you anytime!

1

Alpacas are members of the camelid family, along with dromedary camels, Bactrian camels, llamas, vicuñas, and guanacos.

ith feet dangling and a vast amount of open air beneath me, a thought carved its way through my panic: *Is this really living your best life, Amelia Jean?*

"Stay calm, sweetie, and don't wiggle around too much." Mom's voice sounded deliberately steady as it bounced off the canyon walls. I carefully tipped forward and peered down at the base of the cliff, where she and my two older brothers were waiting for me to descend.

Big mistake.

The height, the nothingness surrounding me—my head started spinning like I'd just stepped off an amusement ride rather than being strapped into some sort of carabiner pulley system. On second thought, the two had a lot in common. Both made my heart pound uncontrollably. And both were activities favored by the rest of my family.

I'd been assigning fear ratings (on a scale of one to ten) for years. My ranking system started when I'd nearly been swept away by an undercurrent in the Pacific Ocean on the day the Amundsen family decided to learn how to surf. Since then, among other things, we'd gone glacier climbing in Alaska (fear rating seven); paragliding on the Oregon coast (fear rating six—which would've been a nine, but I'd ridden tandem with a pilot); backcountry camping in Yellowstone (fear rating four—which would've been lower, except bears); and white-water rafting in Wyoming, New Mexico, and Wisconsin (varying fear ratings from three to eight, depending on the classification of the rapids).

My family bounced around. *A lot.* The common thread was always adventure. And don't get me wrong, adventure could be fun, but it also presented ample opportunity for me and my stupid fears to mess things up. Like when my family bought tickets for the Skywalk in Arizona but had to skip it because I was too scared to go out on the glass bridge extending over the rim of the Grand Canyon. Or, worse, a year ago when a team of mountain rescuers was called in because I'd frozen halfway up a via ferrata. They had to use ropes to pull me out from above because I was too terrified to continue climbing the iron rungs bolted into the side of the mountain.

Even then, I'd only given the via ferrata a fear rating of nine. This latest expedition warranted a solid nine and a half. And, as hard as I was fighting to keep it together, I was losing the battle. The air whooshed out of my lungs. I inhaled rapidly, but everything I brought in was pushed out twice as fast by the alarm coursing through my body.

"Your mom is right," Dad's voice rang out from up above. "Just stay calm. You're perfectly safe as long as you don't somehow manage to slip upside down and out of the harness."

Terrific. Now I had images in my head of me, I don't know, sneeze-rolling myself into a hundred-foot tumble and splatting on the already-red rocks below. Calm was no longer an option—if it ever had been.

I'd somehow mustered enough courage to complete two shorter rappels earlier today. But on those, all I had to do was slowly feed rope through the rappel device hooked to my harness as I walked down a rock wall, backward and in a seated position.

This was my first free rappel, where the cliff wall curved inward, and I was left hanging midair to complete the descent. Nothing to brace my feet against. Nothing but air.

"C'mon, Amelia," yelled Neil, my oldest brother. "YOLO, right? You've got this." The words were encouraging, but the huff of annoyance that followed was not.

"I was scared, too," David chimed in. It was nice of him to say so, but I knew it wasn't true. "Keep threading the rope through the belay device," he continued, "and try not to look down."

But I already had—looked down, that is. And because of it, I couldn't control my breathing and my heart wouldn't stop drumming in my ears.

After the embarrassing evac on the via ferrata, my parents gradually reexposed me to hair-raising situations. They took me on amusement park rides with increasingly larger drops. Next, a trip to the top of the Empire State Building. Then the glass Skydeck Ledge of the Willis Tower in Chicago. Somehow, they managed to shuffle these experiences in between other Amundsen Family Adventure Challenges. Like I wouldn't notice what they were up to.

Then this adventure challenge was picked—completing a free rappel—and, well, I'd seen the looks exchanged behind my back. They weren't sure I could do it, and I hated ruining everyone else's fun. I hated being a disappointment.

So, I'd acted excited, even though I wasn't. I pretended it was no big deal, even though the thought of being back in a harness ran ice through my veins. And now, here I was, scared out of my mind again, and with nothing remotely close to an iron rung to cling to this time.

My hands were clammy. I felt cold all over despite the scorching Utah sun.

"Amelia?" Mom called again.

I couldn't answer, not with the tremor that started in my lower jaw and extended to my toes.

"Honey, it's all right," Mom shouted. "Take all the time you need."

Not meaning to, I glanced down again, and that's when my sweaty hands slipped off the rope. For a terrifying second, the rope ran freely through the rappel device and I fell. I thought I was going to *die*. Seriously, I did. My heart skipped a beat and a scream exploded from my lungs. Then the safety cord tightened abruptly, and I jerked to a stop.

"Whoa!" David called up from below. "Always keep at least one hand on the rope."

I knew that. But when something scared me, all bets were off. And, just like when I'd frozen up on the via ferrata, I was petrified.

"It's okay," Dad called down with forced cheerfulness. "You're not in any danger, but you're going to need to release friction on the autoblock before you can start moving again."

I heard what Dad was saying, but my head was buzzing. He might as well have been speaking a foreign language, considering the way my mind refused to make sense of anything. The concentration required to adjust my equipment was 100 percent out of the question.

"You've got to be kidding me." Neil groaned. He wasn't talking to me, but his voice wafted up. "How long is she going to be stuck this time?"

Air escaped my mouth and lungs in rapid little spurts.

Mom's voice broke through the noise inside my head. "Amelia Jean, take deep breaths and listen to your father. He'll talk you through this."

"Right." Dad's voice came from above. "You'll need to slide the safety cord down the rope to loosen the autoblock, and then you'll be able to feed rope through your rappel device again."

I'd practiced this with him countless times before ever swinging over the side of a ledge, but it all seemed like gibberish now. Instead of sliding the safety cord, I relocked both hands in a death grip around the rope. There was no way I was removing either of them to release tension on the autoblock. Right then, the autoblock was my best friend. Why on earth would I want to mess with it?

I held myself perfectly still, doing everything I could to reduce the sway in the rope and harness. For a moment that dragged on forever, no one said anything. And then my family started to have a conversation, an argument really, about me. Their voices spanned the height of a canyon wall as they ignored the fact that I was stuck halfway between them.

"I told you it was too soon," Mom grumbled at Dad. "Now what?"

"This is ridiculous," Neil said. "It's not like she's rappelling off Mount Thor."

"I could go for help," David offered.

"You're not going anywhere." Mom's voice was scathing. But I knew her irritation was with me, not my brother.

"Yeah, if anyone's going for help, it should be me," Neil said. "I'm older."

"Both of you stay where you're at," Dad called down. "Just give me a minute while I rig up another anchor."

I tuned out their voices and passed the time with my eyes firmly closed. I wasn't going to take any chances. When I opened them again, Dad was dangling in the air beside me. "Hey there, kiddo," he said.

He sounded happy, but there was regret in his eyes. I knew he was worried he'd pushed me into this, even though I'd said it would be fine. A part of him must've known all along that when the rest of the family had been pumped for this adventure, I'd been pretending.

"I'm going to help you finish the descent, okay?"

I breathed in sharply through my nose, then shook my head.

"It's our best option, Amelia Jean. Unless you want to

release the autoblock and continue on by yourself?" he asked hopefully.

I clamped my eyes shut again. The air I'd sucked in drained through my quivering lips.

Dad sighed. "I didn't think so. We'll do it the hard way, then." He finagled the ropes and carabiners, unlocking and locking, tying and untying . . . I couldn't watch. Next thing I knew, he had me off my rappel system and hooked onto his. I buried my head in his shoulder while he lowered us both to the canyon floor.

Mom folded me into her arms as Dad unclipped us both.

Half-hearted cheers rang out among my family members. "Congratulations, Amundsens. Free rappel challenge unlocked," Dad said, like I hadn't just wimped out and failed them all. He held out his hands. "Give me some!" He high-fived with my brothers, and then my mom. When he came to me, I barely lifted my head.

"Gonna keep me hanging, are you?"

When I shrugged and kept my arms planted at my sides, he drummed his fingers playfully on my helmet. "You'll finish on your own next time," he whispered in my ear.

I smiled weakly and nodded my head. "Yeah, next time," I said. Then I choked down a small amount of bile rising in my throat.

Alpacas are the smallest members of the camel family.

Dad spent the first forty-five years of his life not really living, or so he says. He and Mom were both corporate lawyers in their "previous lives." One day, he had this grand idea— every time he and Mom had a bad day at work, they would scribble something they'd rather be doing on a piece of paper and toss it in a giant mason jar. Then, when they had enough money saved, they'd sell everything, hit the road, and start living their "best lives." Nothing as conventional as a road map even. They'd simply draw a slip from the jar and see which way it took them.

That day, the day they packed their bags for adventure and loaded the family into the yellow travel trailer, was five years ago. I was seven. David was nine, and Neil was ten. A lot had changed since then.

For one thing, when my parents bought the trailer, they called it "Winne" (short for Winnebago). It had started out shiny and new. It was dented now, had national park stickers slapped all over it, and had been renamed the Gnarly Banana by my two older brothers.

For another, our lifestyle had started out as the coolest vacation ever. Lately, however, I'd been feeling like an outsider in my own family. While everyone else was pushing the limits, I was doing all I could to keep from falling on my face. And sometimes, I couldn't even manage that.

I was ashamed of how freaked out I'd been by the free rappel. My family had to notice the way I'd moped around since we'd returned to the trailer. But, as usual, they pretended not to notice. They probably thought talking about my fears would only give rise to bigger ones.

"Time for a new slip!" Mom announced after the dinner dishes were cleared from the table. Dad passed her the Adventure Jar, and then ceremoniously beat a drumroll on the trailer wall.

My knees knocked with David's beneath the flimsy table that doubled as my bed. The Formica top popped right off at night, and the cushions came down. My brothers' bunks were at the back of the trailer. My parents slept on the full-sized bed up front.

"Amelia Jean, will you do the honors?" Mom asked, then held the jar out to me. It was obvious she wanted me to still feel included after I'd flubbed today's challenge. Not that she'd say so. What else was there to do but play along? I obligingly dipped my fingers in.

We'd gone through quite a few slips the past five years. Not all adventures were scary—like visiting the Alamo in San Antonio, searching for precious gemstones at Crater of Diamonds State Park in Arkansas (we didn't find any), or even riding a fan boat through a swamp in New Orleans (although no one told me about the gators until after the tour was over).

I had to stretch my fingers way down to the bottom of the jar to retrieve a folded piece of paper. When I opened it up, Mom's neat handwriting popped out at me, proclaiming the next challenge. "Ski a Black Diamond," I read aloud.

I scrunched up my nose. That one would never do. It was the end of July. We hadn't seen snow for months and wouldn't for at least a few more. Relieved (because I knew enough about skiing to know that I'd be a disaster waiting to happen on the steepest, most hazardous type of ski slope), I refolded the slip and prepared to swap it out for a new one. But Dad stopped me. "Whoa, let's talk about it before you toss that fish back in the pond."

That was strange. It's not like this was the first time anyone had drawn a challenge that wasn't a good match for the time of year. We'd always returned the slip to the jar and then drawn a different one. Then there was the weird eye contact Mom and Dad were making. But, parents—who understood them?

Mom broke the silence by letting out a breath I hadn't realized she'd been holding. She said, "Well, that's fortunate."

"Serendipitous, I'd say," added Dad.

I glanced at Neil and David, wondering if they were any more clued in than I was. Something was definitely up. But my brothers' smiling faces revealed nothing. Either they were too stoked about the upcoming Amundsen Adventure to notice our parents' odd behavior, or they were keeping secrets from me, too. I felt a familiar stab of jealousy. The two of them were a team—my fearless brothers, ready to conquer the world. And then there was me. It was fine. I got it. They had the same interests and all. But occasionally, I wished we could be a trio instead.

"Are you thinking what I'm thinking?" Neil asked.

"Oh yeah," David responded. "Best skiing in the US is in—"

"Colorado!" they hooted in unison, drawing out the syllables of the state's name like Col-lor-RAD-oh.

I narrowed my eyes. Even though I was very different from my brothers, there was no denying that we all looked alike. Everyone said so. The three of us were tall for our ages. We'd all inherited Mom's pale skin and plum-round cheeks, and

Dad's dark hair and eyebrows. That's really what people meant when they commented on the family resemblance. We three Amundsen offspring had the same distinctly dark, thick, and expressive eyebrows. And right now, my brothers had theirs elevated in exclamatory arches. Nah, they weren't in on any secrets, they were just excited.

"Kids . . ." Mom started, and then paused.

Here we go, I thought. The pause. Mom always paused when she had something important to say. I kicked straight across at David's shin, and then at Neil's where he sat catty-corner from me.

David shot up in his cushioned seat, and Neil a second after. "Ouch, not cool, Amelia Jean. What was that for?"

"Pay attention," I hissed, and tipped my head in Mom's direction. They could celebrate our next challenge later. I wanted to know what was up with our parents.

"Okay," Mom continued. "So, when we calculated funds for our travels, we didn't quite take into account how much our grocery bills would increase over the years."

I glared at my brothers with their bottomless stomachs. Mom would never come right out and say it, but I knew what she meant. They ate more, *a lot more*, than they did five years ago.

"Plus," she said, "we haven't been economical in reaching our various travel destinations."

Dad cut in, "Your mom's right. We've been zigzagging across the country instead of condensing the miles spent on the road. The extra gas money adds up."

"Are you saying we're broke?" Neil asked.

"No, not broke, exactly," Dad said. "We just need to be smarter about how we spend money. And—"

"And what?" I asked. An uneasy feeling caused my stomach muscles to tighten.

"And your mom and I will need to find jobs, so the three of you will have to go back to a brick-and-mortar school for a little while."

Our way of life hadn't allowed for public schooling. We'd taken some online classes over the years, but not everywhere we traveled had the best Wi-Fi. Most of our education had been given on the road—we stopped at bookstores and purchased books on Dad's assigned reading lists. Mom covered math and science.

My stomach relaxed, and I sat up straighter in my seat. My memories of school were of circle time and playing freeze tag on the blacktop at recess, and of Ms. Laskey, the school librarian, who always smelled like fresh cotton and called everyone "honey" in a thick Southern accent. My memories of school were nice and were tied to memories of a home that wasn't on wheels and had wild rosebushes lining the path to a front door.

Our old front door had been painted yellow, like the Gnarly Banana, but was far more welcoming.

"Not public school, nuh-uh," Neil said. "No way are we going back to spending Six Crappy Hours of Our Lives bored to death inside a brick building. How are we supposed to live life to the fullest when we're imprisoned by the system? Eh?" My oldest brother knew exactly how to play our father—by throwing some of Dad's favorite verbiage right back at him.

Dad pushed a fair amount of air out through his nose.

Our education had been one without schedules and "the grind" Dad ranted against. In many ways, homeschooling had bought our family freedom. Plus, my parents said we were able to learn at a quicker pace because so much of traditional school was centered around organizing groups of students and getting everyone on the same page.

"Can't we keep homeschooling ourselves?" David pressed.

My eyes shot to Dad. Were my brothers wearing him down? I hadn't realized just how much I liked the idea of going back to school until there was a chance it might slip away.

Luckily, Dad didn't bite. "I'm sorry, it's not a choice," he said firmly, and there was a clip to his voice that wasn't usually there. Not anymore, anyway. Not since we'd started living life out of the Adventure Jar.

"It's only temporary," Mom added. "Your dad and I need to

bring in some extra income while we figure out our finances. Neither of us will have time to manage your curriculums while we're working, so, public school it is."

"But—" Neil protested.

"*But* it'll only be for half a school year or so," Mom cut him off. "Until winter break."

Dad picked up the thread. "And, by then, we'll have completed the Black Diamond Challenge and can move on to the next. It's not like we're going to fall right back into the rat race. No one is going to be 'imprisoned by the system.' We have our adventure challenge. We'll fulfill it, and then we'll move on. Just like always. You see, serendipitous." The more Dad talked, the more he seemed to be convincing himself that this would all work out fine.

"You know, 'The wide world is all about you: You can fence yourselves in, but you cannot forever fence it out.' Who said that?" Dad asked.

My brothers and I had cut our teeth on *The Hobbit* and the Lord of the Rings trilogy. Quoting the author of the most epic adventure novels ever was a common pastime in the Amundsen family.

"J. R. R. Tolkien." Neil said the name with reverence. He and David exchanged a look that said they were relenting to the idea of going back to school.

"That's right. We may not like it, but our fence is coming

down. At least for a little while. Middle school for Amelia Jean, high school for Neil and David. It'll be good for the three of you to have some shared experiences with people your own age. In fact . . ." As Dad trailed off, the expression on his face brightened like something pleasant had just dawned on him.

"In fact, what, dear?" Mom asked, no doubt confused by the dopey grin on Dad's face.

"Colorado," Dad said while purposely nodding like the state's name was supposed to mean something.

"Suuure," Mom said slowly. "Colorado seems like a logical choice. It has some of the best skiing in the world, and it's not too far from here—it shares a border with the state of Utah."

Dad continued to nod. "Right? And how many times have we said it's a pity our kids have never met their cousin? Doesn't this seem like a prime opportunity? Serendipitous even?"

"Would you stop saying that?" Mom jokingly chided Dad for his persistent use of the word *serendipitous*. I remembered it from one of Dad's vocabulary assignments. It meant something that happened by chance in a happy or beneficial way.

"Fair enough, but tell me what you think," Dad pressed.

"Well . . . the younger Catherine does live in Winterland, close to a world-class ski resort." Her gaze drifted away from Dad. For a moment she seemed to contemplate what that meant. "But I don't know . . ."

"Why not? It's perfect!" Dad crooned. "She's the same age as Amelia Jean. Who better to shepherd Amelia back into the school system than family?"

Now he had my full attention. My dad's sister and her daughter were both named Catherine. My cousin Catherine lived with her grandmother because my aunt Catherine had left when she was a baby and now lived somewhere in Europe. Every few years Dad got an email from my aunt, so we knew she was still alive. But she never came back to visit. And even though we sent a birthday card to my cousin Catherine every year, we'd never actually met her.

"Won't that be awkward?" Mom asked. "I mean, the poor girl was abandoned by *your* sister. And she lives with her dad's mother, right? We've never received a response to any of the mail we've sent, so we have no idea if she wants anything to do with us."

I held my breath. On one hand, I'd always been intrigued by the cousin I'd never met. What if it turned out we were two peas in a pod, like my brothers? Then I wouldn't always feel like the odd one out. On the other hand, Mom was probably right. It might be awkward.

Dad shook his head. "Maybe at first. But anything worth doing usually is."

"I guess," Mom said. "Winterland it is."

Butterflies erupted in my stomach, but it wasn't a bad tingling. Not the kind I get when I'm about to freak out. It was more nervous anticipation—like the future held the promise of something sweet and good. "Serendipitous," I whispered so Mom wouldn't hear. Going back to school might be exactly what I needed. A chance to meet my cousin. A chance to make friends and feel like I belonged. A chance to participate in activities that didn't involve dangerous mountains. That was, at least until the slopes opened . . .

The tension had gone out of Dad's dark eyebrows. And he'd gotten through to my brothers with that Tolkien quote. I could tell by their slumped shoulders that the fight had drained out of them. Mom was never easy to read. Unlike me, she stayed calm and composed no matter what. But even though my family seemed resigned to this big change, I could tell they were all scared. Even Mom.

I couldn't believe how the tables had turned. While I'd been biting my nails through each challenge, they really had been living their "best lives." Now they were afraid that the Amundsen Adventure Jar Lifestyle might be coming to an end just as I was feeling excited for what lay ahead. What if my happiness always meant their misery, and vice versa? I worried we would never be in sync. I didn't worry long, though, because my anticipation for going back to school and living in one place for more than a few days outweighed everything. For once, I couldn't wait to hit the road.

3

Alpacas are indigenous to South America and have been domesticated for thousands of years.

WELCOME TO COLORFUL COLORADO, the sign read as we crossed the state line. And it didn't lie. The views along the sometimes straight, sometimes curvy highway were constantly changing. Red rocks, purple mountains, green trees, blue skies, and fields of gold. We were greeted by some of the prettiest landscapes I'd ever seen, and I'd seen more than my fair share.

My brothers were uncharacteristically quiet as we drove. They were still brooding over school. Normally we'd stop at scenic overlooks or small-town museums along the way, but not this time. Winterland High and Winterland Middle were (serendipitously?) scheduled to start the next day, and there was a ton of stuff to do before then. So, we headed straight for the place where we'd park the Gnarly Banana for the foreseeable future.

The Stargazer RV Park, located on the outskirts of Winterland, wasn't very full. We had our pick of campsites. We chose a secluded one at the back of the park—one surrounded by evergreen trees and aspens. My brothers and I hopped out of the truck cab to explore while our parents got the Gnarly Banana situated.

I greedily breathed in the sharp scent of pine and the musky smell of forest undergrowth. My brothers darted in and out of the trees and scrambled over boulders, their bad moods obviously lifting. It felt amazing to be outdoors after being pent up in the truck all morning.

My parents had a long list of things to do once we'd disconnected the Gnarly Banana from the truck and connected it to the RV park's water, electricity, and sewer hookups. I begged them to bump "Contact Catherine" to the top of the list.

"I can't believe I don't have a phone number for my own niece," Dad said, then he slightly clenched his jaw.

"At least we have an address," Mom said. "We can swing by on the way to register the kids for school. Knock two things off our list with one trip."

My family piled back into the quad cab truck. It moved a great deal faster without the Gnarly Banana dragging behind.

Squashed in the back seat again between David and Neil, I bounced my knees on the floorboard. I couldn't wait to meet Catherine, but that didn't mean I wasn't nervous.

Catherine and her grandmother lived at the top of a steep, winding drive fifteen minutes away from the RV park. Their cabin was made of enormous round logs and an angled roof. It was small but impressive. It was solid—like, if you were one of the three little pigs and the big bad wolf was coming, *this* was the house you should choose. Even the front door seemed sturdier than most. When Dad rapped his knuckles on it (because there was no doorbell to be found), the sound was deep and echoey. It sounded nothing at all like a knock on the flimsy door of the Gnarly Banana.

We waited patiently on the front stoop until the silence grew uncomfortable. Then Dad tried again. Still no one answered. "Should we go?" Dad asked.

"David and I can wait around," Neil offered. "See if they come back."

Mom checked the time on her phone. "Nice try," she said. "You know the office at the high school closes soon."

Neil grinned sheepishly in reply.

"We're registering the three of you for school today one way or another. We'll leave a note instead."

The note explained who we were and where we were staying.

It had Dad's cell phone number printed neatly at the bottom. It also mentioned that I'd be starting seventh grade with Catherine the next day. Dad wedged the note in the crack between the door and the frame.

I tried not to be disappointed as we drove away. Only one more day and I'd get to meet Catherine anyway. She might even call before then.

Since we were short on time, Mom dropped Dad and my brothers off at the high school and she and I continued to the middle school. As we pulled into the parking lot, I noticed it was larger than the one-story brick building where I'd gone to elementary school. It was newer, too. It was modern-looking with geometric-shaped walls painted in earth tones—deep greens, browns, maroons, and cloudy blues.

I wanted to get a good look around inside, but the main office was less than ten feet from the front door. As soon as we entered the room, we found a woman sitting at a desk—her nameplate said she was Ms. Horton, and that she was the attendance secretary.

Mom explained who we were and why we were here. I was so eager to be enrolling in a school with students my age that it didn't dampen my spirits any when Ms. Horton turned up her nose at me. At least, not much.

"Homeschooled," she said distastefully, like my parents had

done me some great disservice by not having me in public schools all these years.

That's when I noticed she had squinty eyes, even though she wore glasses, thin greasy bangs, and was clutching a jar full of multicolored gel pens that she seemed awfully protective of. Out of nerves, I'd started fiddling with them as Mom introduced us. The woman snatched the jar away and repositioned the pens on her desk, out of my reach.

"Do you have *any* records?" She looked me up and down. "Seventh grade, you say? Hmm . . . You know, she might need to be bumped back a grade or two . . . You should probably investigate registering her at the elementary school instead."

A grade or two?! I'd be a giant compared to the elementary school kids. I nearly buckled with dread. And whenever I got nervous, I acted strangely. I giggled even though none of this was funny. I tugged at a strand of hair that had loosened itself from my ponytail. Worst of all, as I pictured myself towering over and frightening a kindergartner on the playground, a Lord of the Rings quote bubbled out of me: "'He had imagined himself meeting giants taller than trees, and other creatures even more terrifying.'"

Ms. Horton stared at me like I had a third eye, and I gulped, worried my weird behavior had just sealed my fate.

Luckily, Mom kept her cool. "Seventh grade," she stated again. Then she smiled pertly and handed the woman a stack of papers, including my birth certificate, immunization records, standardized test scores, transcripts, report cards . . . you name it. Mom had come prepared.

Ms. Horton shuffled through the paperwork, hmphed loudly, then said, "I'll have to make copies and speak to the principal, but her test scores are very high. Be aware that further assessment may be required to confirm that we're placing her correctly, but for now I'll enroll Amelia. She can start school with our seventh graders at eight a.m. tomorrow."

Relief washed over me. I pictured myself at a desk, a real desk, not the cramped corner seat in the Gnarly Banana. I'd have people my age to talk to. And I'd get invited to do normal middle school stuff. Like see a movie or grab ice cream over the weekend.

I continued fantasizing about school after we returned to the RV park. My brothers had strung up a hammock and I swung in the breeze, staring up through leaves dappling the big blue sky. I wondered if there was a cozy reading corner in the library, like there had been at my old school. Memories of first grade surfaced in my mind. I remembered safely living out adventures through the stories the school librarian shared and acting them out at recess with my friends. I had loved school. I had *belonged* at school. More than anything, that was what I was hoping to find at Winterland Middle.

"What's with you?" Neil asked. "Why do you look so happy?"

Our parents were knocking the next few items off their list—going into town in search of jobs and food for dinner—and had left me with my brothers.

I swung my legs over the side of the hammock and sat up straight to face him. "Um, did Catherine call while you were with Dad?" Dad had been in such a rush to get back to his to-do list that I hadn't been able to ask him before he and Mom left.

"Don't know," my brother said. "I don't think so."

I felt the same small pang of disappointment that I had when she hadn't answered the door. "No big deal," I said, and forced a smile. "I'll meet her tomorrow."

My family didn't have the time (or money) to shop for new school clothes and supplies. So, before bed, I dusted a bit of Utah sand off a backpack, then filled it with sharpened pencils, crisp lined paper, and an only slightly beat-up purple plastic binder. I gingerly hung the pack on a hook by the door inside the trailer.

I spent most of the night tossing and turning and woke an hour earlier than I needed to. No fairy godmother had turned my rags into a new wardrobe while I slept, so I dug out the least wrinkly T-shirt from my duffel bag—a bright orange one we'd picked up in Yosemite that screamed tourist—and a secondhand pair of knit shorts. The shorts were turquoise, and I knew they didn't match the shirt, but they were the nicest pair I had.

My brothers were still asleep, so I tiptoed to the back of the trailer. Waking up early was worth it to have the bathroom all to myself, and no one banging at the door telling me to hurry up. I showered and then pulled my damp hair into a loose ponytail at the nape of my neck. It was about the only hairstyle I could manage. Even if I'd known how to curl or tease or iron my hair, it wasn't like we had the space for any beauty products in our one tiny bathroom.

Dad was shaking my brothers awake when I slid the door open. I waited since there wasn't room for all of us in the hallway—if you could even call it that. When the path was clear, I grabbed myself some of the milk Mom and Dad had picked up in town and opened a new box of cereal.

Everyone was groggy at breakfast, except me. I scarfed it down and was the first one loaded in the truck. My parents were the next to join me, and when it seemed like my brothers were never going to make it into the vehicle, Mom reached across from the passenger seat and laid on the horn. "They'll make us all late," she said.

Dad had found a job at the market where they'd gone for groceries the night before and his first shift started at nine a.m.

Mom had seen a HELP WANTED sign in the window of a local deli. She wanted to be there when they opened to apply. But first, my parents planned to drive us in today, for "old times' sake" or something like that. After school, I'd ride the bus home, and the high school was close enough that my brothers could walk.

Neil and David eventually made it into the truck. Five minutes later, when we arrived at the high school, they poured like molasses out of the cab and onto the sidewalk. They looked even more alike than usual, with their heads drooped at the exact same angle and their hands shoved deep in their pockets. I wasn't the only one who noticed they were moping. "Give them a few days," Mom said as Dad pulled the truck away from the curb. "They'll get used to it."

Me, on the other hand, I marched through the front doors of Winterland Middle School with my head held high, hopeful. The sun was shining on the angled exterior walls today, and in through the tall glass windows, making cool shadows on the floor. The hallways were bright, and I was anxious to see more of the building than just the front office.

First stop, my locker. Ms. Horton had circled it on a map of the school she'd given me the day before. She'd written the combination down, and instructions on how to open it. I'd opened a zillion padlocks before, so I wasn't worried.

On my way there, I made eye contact with a girl coming my

direction and smiled. I thought maybe it was the light glinting in her eyes through the skylight, or maybe she was brooding over the start of school like my brothers, but she didn't smile back. I waved, and the look on her face grew even more sour.

I shrugged it off and carried on. A boy was standing with his back to me. He was talking to a girl facing my direction. I flashed her a toothy smile, too. She said something to the boy, and he whirled around. They both scrutinized my outfit, my shoes, my hair, my makeup (or lack thereof) before meeting my eyes. I wasn't sure who to focus on, so my gaze darted between them. The boy spun back around, quickly losing interest. The girl shot me a withering smile and resumed talking to the boy.

I sucked in a deep breath and picked up speed. My locker was only a few steps ahead. As I fiddled with the combination, it was like someone opened the floodgates. Students came pouring in. It dawned on me that I'd arrived before most everyone else. And everyone else was arriving at almost the same time. Walking down the near empty hallway to get to my locker had been easy peasy, but now . . . the number of bodies, the noise, the commotion . . . my head was spinning. I couldn't concentrate on my locker combination.

"Excuse me," someone said. I looked all around only to jolt a little when I discovered the voice was coming from below me.

A boy was kneeling by my feet. I could only see the top of his head. "Um, I can't get to my locker," he said. "Would you move?"

"Uh, um, I . . ." I couldn't force any meaningful words out of my mouth.

He popped to his feet, snatched the paper out of my hand, spun the combo, and my locker door swung open.

I stood back, dumbstruck, while he then proceeded to open his own locker. He finished doing what he needed to in like two seconds, then he slammed it shut and bolted.

"Thanks," I called after him. "My name's Amelia!" I shouted, but he never looked back.

Heading to my first class didn't go any better. I was starting to fear that my brothers had been right. Jumping back into school after five years away wasn't giving me a sense of belonging. Not even close. So far it was more like diving into a pool of sharks. Which was something I'd experienced firsthand at Mandalay Bay Shark Reef Aquarium in Las Vegas (fear rating seven). On a side note, it must've been a particularly dark day for one of my parents to think "swimming with (actual) sharks" was preferable to their day jobs.

At least when we'd been snorkeling at the aquarium, I hadn't brushed up against any of the leering creatures. That wasn't the case at my new school. I was swimming right among them— knocking shoulders and being pushed aside.

Still, I didn't give up *right away*. I smiled and waved at everyone I encountered. It was a tactic that had worked well in first grade. But in seventh, it just made me feel increasingly stupid when no one treated me friendly in return.

When the other middle schoolers did make eye contact with me, their expressions said I'd already been dismissed before they'd even given me a chance. Halfway to my first-period class, I let my head droop and I shoved my hands into my pockets.

And then there was the fact that my last days at Ralston Elementary had been spent with kids who occasionally still wet their pants. I couldn't help but notice that I was sharing crowded hallway space with students in desperate need of deodorant, and a few who even shaved. School was nothing at all like my memories.

Because I'd dropped my gaze to the shadows on the floor, I accidentally bumped into a boy. He was taller than most everyone else in middle school. Maybe he was one of the eighth graders? Of course, I was about the same height, and I was in seventh, so who knew? His hair was clipped close to his head except for the top, which was long and swept forward like a cresting wave.

"I . . . I'm sorry," I stammered.

"Watch it," he snarled, and then moved on like I wasn't

worth his time. In fact, that seemed to be everyone's response to me—I wasn't worth their time. I staggered on, up the stairs, down another hallway, and at last found my way to room 203. Along the way, no one said hello. No one offered to point me in the right direction. I felt like a fool for ever thinking I'd fit in.

Then things got even worse. Because I was new to Winterland, my first-period social studies teacher, Mr. Roybal, made me stand to introduce myself. "Amelia," he said, "you weren't by chance named after the famous aviator Amelia Earhart, were you?"

"That's right," I croaked out, with as much poise as a giraffe. "I was." I didn't mention that my older brother Neil was named after Neil Armstrong, the first person to walk on the moon. Or that David was named after David Livingstone, a famous nineteenth-century explorer. Everyone seemed to think I was odd enough already.

"You must be very brave," Mr. Roybal said with a wink. I knew he meant well, but that's not the sort of thing you want someone to announce to a room of strangers. Especially when you're worried you can't live up to it.

"So, tell us, where are you from?" he said.

"Um . . ." It was a standard question. I'm sure most people would have no trouble answering it. But I wasn't most people. "Uh . . ." I wrung my hands in front of me. I had no good, concise answer. And then, thanks again to my family's obsession with J. R. R. Tolkien, I blurted out the only thing that came to mind—a quote my family had framed and hanging over the kitchen sink in our home on wheels. "Um, 'not all those who wander are lost.'"

Mr. Roybal chuckled appreciatively, but the students stared back at me stone-faced. A few of them shot knowing glances at one another, like I'd just confirmed their most unflattering thoughts about me.

"A traveler, then. So, you're brave *and* adventurous," Mr. Roybal continued. "You know, you and Catherine Winter might have a lot in common—beyond having a famous namesake. What do you say, Catherine; are you willing to be an ambassador for our new student?"

Catherine? Could it be? It felt like I'd been tossed a lifeline, at last. But I had no idea what my cousin looked like. And what was that part about a famous namesake? I must've furrowed my brow because my teacher pointed to a girl with white-blonde hair seated a row in front of me. He explained, "Winterland was named after Catherine's great-great-grandfather, the founder of our town—so you both were named after industrious individuals."

I'd known my cousin's last name was Winter, but not that her ancestor had given the town its name. Somehow, that made me even more nervous to meet her. She had deep, solid roots

· 33 ·

here. For almost as far back as I could remember, I'd been a tumbleweed blowing in the wind.

As Catherine slowly swiveled toward me, I could hardly contain myself. I was so anxious to finally make a connection. But why hadn't she said anything when I introduced myself to the class? Was she embarrassed by me? Or maybe my family's note had blown away in the wind, and she had no idea who I was, and that the two of us had far more in common than Mr. Roybal had implied? *Yes, that must be it.*

I could almost feel the hope and anxiety pooling in my eyes as I stared expectantly at my cousin. Would she know who I was? Would she like me? She resembled pictures I'd seen of my aunt Catherine when she and Dad were young. She looked nothing like any of the rest of us. She was fair to our dark and had been bestowed with enviably normal eyebrows. To my bewilderment, however, they were drawn together, almost in a scowl. "Catherine was my mother's name," she said.

I recoiled. Why did she seem . . . hostile?

The look on her face said she knew exactly who I was, but that my presence in her school—her town, apparently—was unwelcome. There was no doubt in my mind that she had seen our note and had decided not to call.

My heart plummeted. I thought it might be awkward meeting her, but not like this. Was it because I wore the wrong clothes and my hair wasn't styled like all the other girls in the class? Did she not want anyone to know we were related, or was there something more to it?

Despite this, my cousin apparently wasn't the type of student to ignore a teacher's request. Finally, she answered Mr. Roybal's question by saying, "Sure, I'll be her ambassador." Then, speaking to me, she said, "Call me Cat," before whirling back around to face the front of the room.

Mr. Roybal blinked a few times as if trying to discern where the sudden tension in the air had come from. But he quickly glossed over it by clearing his throat. He moved on to handing out a syllabus for the school year.

During the remainder of the period, a few eyes drifted in my direction, but most of the other students didn't seem all that interested. Not the sporty girls with their messy buns and laser-cut leggings, or the preppy girls wearing plaid skirts and makeup, or the cute-casual group in oversized T-shirts and skinny jeans.

I snuck a glance at Catherine—er, Cat—whenever I could. I replayed her reaction in my head. Was it possible she hadn't been as irritated as I thought? Or maybe she was just an angry person in general.

I couldn't quite peg her. Her athletic build, sweat shorts, and T-shirt said sporty, but her hair was slicked neat, and she was wearing lip gloss. Now that she wasn't glaring at me, the muscles in her face had relaxed. I noticed that she smiled easily— at other people. No, something had definitely been off about the way she'd responded to me.

As far as I knew, I hadn't done anything to offend her. But if my own cousin didn't want me here, who would? There weren't any other girls wearing thrift store outfits that were wrinkly because they came out of a duffel bag stored beneath their bed/ kitchen table. Or any girls who were like mountains compared to the rest. And even though I'd lived with two brothers all my life, the boys seemed even more unrelatable than the girls.

For the last five years, I'd spent every day primarily with only four other people—Mom, Dad, Neil, and David. Now I was surrounded by an entire class of kids my age. But I felt more isolated than I had in some of the most remote places on the planet. So much for my high hopes that school would be a place I felt like I belonged.

I slumped in my seat. Maybe that was for the best. This school, these classmates, they were just another fleeting experience in a long list of Amundsen adventures. Fitting in, making friends—that would only mean there'd be people to miss when we packed up and left. At least, that's what I tried to tell myself. Deep down, I knew I was scared. I was going to be as big a flop in middle school as I was at doing anything daring.

There are no wild alpacas.

The hallway after first period was just as daunting as before. I wanted to stop, take out my schedule and my map to see where I was headed next, but the flow of students carried me down the corridor. And Cat was busy talking to a group of friends. I didn't want to ask her and give her any more reason to be annoyed with me.

I just needed a few minutes to myself. A few minutes to breathe and recover from the disappointing blows the morning kept dealing me. Then I saw the library. I waded through the laughing, chattering, scuffling bodies, ducked inside, and was immediately enveloped by quiet.

It was such a relief to be out of the crowded, noisy halls. A part of me knew I didn't have time to hang around. My next class would be starting soon. But a larger part couldn't bear to leave behind the sanctuary I'd discovered, not yet.

Unfortunately, there wasn't a couch and cozy reading corner. No colorful mural on the wall. Mostly rows of shelves and long tables. I wandered down a narrow row, thankful for the seclusion the stacks of books provided. The row of shelves led to a chair and a window with a view of trees and mountain peaks. It was the first inviting thing I'd seen since arriving at Winterland Middle. So, I sat down, and I got lost in that view.

I don't know how long I sat there. I sat there until a woman with a soft voice and a dimply smile touched me on the shoulder and said, "Do you have a pass, dear?"

Of course, I didn't. I remembered back to first grade and the passes students had to wear around their necks to use the bathroom. "Like a necklace?" I asked.

Her dimples faded. "Not exactly. Wandering around the school without permission isn't permitted. I'm afraid you'll have to go to the office. Explain what happened to Ms. Horton. She can give you a slip to show your second-period teacher."

"Ms. Horton?" I groaned inwardly.

"That's right."

At least the halls were less overwhelming now that the passing period was over and class was in session. When I arrived at the front office, Ms. Horton was on the phone, taking notes with one of her gel pens. She locked eyes with me, and her lips pursed, then tipped downward at the corners. "Guess who just showed up?" she said into the receiver. "Uh-uh, I think Principal Stinger should see her before I send her to class."

The attendance secretary didn't speak right away after hanging up the phone. If she wanted to make me sweat, she succeeded. I shuffled my feet on the carpet and bit my lip nervously as I waited.

Finally, Ms. Horton said, "That was your second-period teacher. I called her as soon as I received her attendance and saw that you'd been marked absent. So, did you get lost, or do you think you're so important that it isn't necessary to show up for class?"

"I, um, I guess, I lost track of time," I said. "I didn't know I needed a pass. I was in the library?"

"Is that a question?" Ms. Horton said curtly.

"What?"

"Were you in the library, or weren't you?"

"I was."

"Why?"

"I don't know."

"Uh-huh." Ms. Horton slapped a hand on her desk as she rose to her feet. "I don't get paid enough to do this job," she mumbled, and then, "C'mon. Let's go see Principal Stinger."

Ms. Horton herded me toward an open door at the back of the room. I'd only been in a principal's office once in my life—when I turned seven and I was called down for my birthday pencil. I'd been excited then, but as I neared the threshold now, my feet were like lead. I could hardly move forward.

Ms. Horton pointed to a chair beside the door. "Sit!" she commanded.

I was happy to oblige. Anything to delay seeing the principal.

Ms. Horton knocked on the door and then entered. "I have that new girl I was telling you about," I could hear her say through the open door. "Apparently, she's having trouble adjusting already. She went to the library instead of her second-period class."

I strained my ears but could only hear one side of the conversation. Whatever the principal said, Ms. Horton didn't seem pleased by it. "Yes, I suppose she's missed enough class already . . . Yes, it can be dealt with later. I just thought . . . Okay."

Ms. Horton pulled the door shut behind her on the way out. She marched to her desk and scribbled a note. Straight backed and stiff armed, she held it out to me. "Take this to your teacher."

I moved to take the slip, but she held it tightly wedged

between her fingers. "However, just because Principal Stinger can't see you at the moment, doesn't mean this is over."

I gulped and she let the pass slide into my hand.

On the plus side, the halls were still empty as I hurried to class. I slunk into second period and handed Ms. Horton's note to the only balding, middle-aged man in the room. He nodded and directed me to an open seat. A seat right next to my cousin.

Cat glared at me. "Where were you?" she hissed as I plopped my bag on the floor and lowered myself into the desk chair.

"Staring out a window," I said.

She shook her head dismissively, then returned to her classwork.

Since Cat was my ambassador, I guess she felt obligated to keep track of me after my little disappearing act. She showed me to the rest of my classes, even the ones she wasn't in. At lunch, she pointed out the trays (I almost passed right by them), and where to pay for my cold chicken tenderloins and hard roll. Naturally, I followed her to her table as well. But she hardly acknowledged my presence the entire time I sat next to her in the cafeteria. And she never once mentioned the note or acknowledged the fact that we were related. In fact, she hardly said anything to me at all. I guess she didn't include friendly conversation as part of her ambassadorial duties.

As the end of the day inched near, I started thinking my

unapproved visit to the library might've been overlooked. That maybe Principal Stinger didn't think it was nearly as big a deal as Ms. Horton had. With each passing hour, my chest felt lighter. Then, five minutes before the final bell rang, the teacher handed me a note addressed to my parents. I opened it, of course.

Mr. & Mrs. Amundsen,

　　After an incident at school today, Principal Stinger has some concerns that Winterland Middle may not be the best environment for Amelia to transition back into the public school system. He would like to interview Amelia and then discuss with you the possibility of transferring her to Winterland Elementary. Please contact me at your earliest convenience to schedule an appointment.

Sincerely,
Ms. Cordelia Horton
Attendance Secretary
Winterland Middle School

My face burned and I couldn't even hold the note steady as I read because I was mad, and I was embarrassed, and it was all I could do not to rip the note in half and toss it in the wastebasket.

Ms. Horton had had it out for me from the get-go and I knew this meeting was her idea. She didn't want me at Winterland Middle in the first place, and now she was going to convince the principal to give me the boot.

When the teacher dismissed the class, I shoved the note to the bottom of my backpack. I bolted from the school building and out into the blinding sunlight. The bus was idling by the curb. I was so worried about the interview—obviously I didn't belong in middle school, but I'd fit in even less in elementary—that it didn't cross my mind to be uneasy about the ride back to the Stargazer RV Park. Why would it? It wasn't like riding down a road in a large vehicle was new to me. I ambled past rows of noisy middle school kids and slid into an open seat near the back. I sidled up to the window and cracked it open. The guys in front of me were complaining about the heat. It was hot, but nothing compared to Utah, or Arizona, or Texas in August.

When the bus started moving, a gentle breeze wafted in. It was pine-scented and calming. As we passed Winterland Ski Resort, I pushed away thoughts of the upcoming interview and my bumpy first day of school and focused on the view outside my window. I spotted patches of wild grasses growing beneath the chairlifts. Wildflowers dotted the mountainside with splashes of white, yellow, and purple. I tried to picture what the ski resort would look like in the dead of winter—grasses and flowers buried by snow, everything stripped of life and color. Thankfully, skiing a black diamond felt a long, safe distance away.

I hadn't realized until that moment how much I'd missed watching the seasons change. I'd experienced summer and fall and winter and spring in various places, but we hadn't stayed in any one location long enough to witness the transformation. As the bus rambled on, I felt a wave of longing. I wanted to watch the tips of leaves turn red and golden in the fall, and bud with new life in the spring. I wanted to experience the scenery changing again, rather than a constant change of scenery.

Lost in thought, I gazed at the trees outside my window. As they blurred by, it hit me that every grove looked alike in Winterland. Every exit off the state highway looked as though it could lead to the Stargazer RV Park. I couldn't tell one mountain peak from another. And everything looked different coming from the opposite direction than the way I'd traveled with Mom and Dad that morning on the way to school.

When I started seeing one building after another pop up outside my bus window, my heart leaped into my throat. The bus was nearing town. *Oh no, I missed my stop!* I thought, followed quickly by, *What will my family think?*

Amundsens were supposed to be proficient at navigation. Over the past few years, I'd been taught how to pay attention to landmarks, and how to find my way out of the wilderness using a compass and a map. Finding your way around a new place was practically a game to my family. But I couldn't even handle something as simple as riding a bus home.

Dad especially wouldn't understand how this could happen. I hated the look he got in his eyes and the way he shook his head in disbelief every time I proved a disappointment. An ache lodged itself inside my rib cage. I was already going to get that look for Ms. Horton's note. I didn't want to get it for missing my bus stop, too.

As the bus neared the center of town (and the market where Dad was now a grocery bagger) one thing became clear—I needed to get off, and fast. If I could somehow find my way back to the Gnarly Banana before my parents got off work, they'd never have to know what a blunder I'd made of my first bus ride.

I hopped out of my seat to exit the bus with a cluster of other middle schoolers. The boy with the wave-top hair—the one I'd bumped into at the start of the day—was directly in front of me. Since my nerves were hitting a crescendo, I was in a hurry to get off. In my haste, I crowded in too close.

Wave-hair boy didn't seem to like the way I stepped onto the pavement, right on his heels. He spun on me, then slowly measured my appearance. It was unnerving the way his gaze moved from my ratty tennis shoes up my body, until it lingered less than an inch above my eyes. Earlier that day, he'd brushed me off like someone swatting away a mosquito. *That* seemed far preferable to the attention he was paying me now.

"Hey!" he said. His voice wasn't friendly. It was the opposite of friendly. The group of kids who'd climbed off before us turned to look.

The boy paused, as if mulling something over in his head. Then, noticing he had everyone's attention, he said, "You have the *thickest* eyebrows I've ever seen on a girl." One of the boys standing near him snorted and a girl off to the right broke into a fit of giggles. A third girl stepped into view, one with hair nearly as white as snow. Cat didn't laugh.

Seemingly encouraged by his audience's reaction, he added, "Seriously, they're hideous—like something furry living on your face. Maybe you *are* lost," he said, referencing the Tolkien quote I'd recited that morning. But he hadn't been in Mr. Roybal's class. Who could've told him about it? *Cat?* That hurt almost more than his insults.

I shrank inside myself, and for a second it seemed like my tormenter was having doubts, like he was going to back off. Then he glanced at Cat. His face steeled in a sneer and he returned his gaze to me. "You are lost, aren't you? So, where did you come from, then? A zoo?"

"Good one, Ryan," said the boy who'd snorted earlier.

My mouth suddenly felt dry, but I couldn't speak, and I couldn't swallow. Was my cousin behind this somehow? Did she really hate me that bad? I searched her eyes for some explanation. Her mouth was pinched tight. She was angry and annoyed and something I couldn't quite read.

I felt confused and scared, but in a different way than when I was staring down the side of a cliff. I had no idea how to react. I had no idea what to say.

My parents had spent the last five years literally trying to teach me not to run from my fears. Neil says FEAR can stand for one of two things: either Forget Everything And Run, or Face Everything And Respond.

I could hear my big brother's voice in my head: "Amundsens are responders, not runners." Not *this* Amundsen. Without saying a word, I spun on my heel and ran. I ran before fear froze me in place and running was no longer an option. I ran and my eyes stung. I wanted to believe it was the wind blowing in my face that blurred my vision. But it wasn't. As I ran away from the insults, and my disastrous first day, the dam broke and the tears flowed freely.

5

There are two types of alpacas: huacaya (pronounced wah-KI-yah) and suri (SOO-ree). Huacaya have fluffy, teddy-bear-like fleece and account for 90 percent of all alpacas. The less common, suri, have long, silky locks of fleece.

The animals first appeared like fuzzy white dots in my distorted image of the field ahead. I thought they might be sheep. But as I drew near, I noticed their necks were too long, and their colors too varied. I stopped running. Using my bright orange T-shirt, I dabbed the wetness from my eyes so I could get a better look.

One of the animals in particular grabbed my attention. He was creamy white. He was munching on hay, and he was looking right at me. His eyes were large, black, and watchful. I still wanted to make it back to the Gnarly Banana before the rest of my family, but both my fear and energy were waning. Now I just felt, I don't know . . . sad, deflated, more than a little bruised on the inside.

I left the side of the road I'd been following and approached the fence. "Hi there," I said softly. The animal didn't move. Up close, he looked even softer and fluffier than I'd imagined. I had an urge to reach through the rails and run fingers through his tufts of fur. Instead, I took off my backpack and rifled through it until I found a forgotten bag of baby carrots I'd packed for a snack.

When my family had gone horseback riding in Montana, I'd learned how to hold the palm of my hand flat when feeding a horse. That way, no fingers would be nibbled along with the treat. I extended my arm through an opening in the fence and held the carrot the way I'd been taught.

The sweet and fuzzy animal took it from me and munched appreciatively on the orange root. Two more adorable creatures joined us by the fence. One was a milky brown, the other the color of caramel. I gave them both carrots as well. Standing there, a peace washed over me that I hadn't felt all day. The feelings of otherness and loneliness I'd been carrying around with me drained away.

I didn't know exactly what the animals were. They looked like llamas but were smaller and had cuter faces. And, unlike horses, their legs narrowed into dainty two-toed feet instead of hooves. While trying to get a better look, I noticed the milky-brown one had a piece of twine wrapped around one of his front legs. His weight was shifted to the opposite leg, like it was bothering him.

I hunched over and stretched my hands through the fence. I tried to grab at the string, but the animal startled and reared back a few inches. "Whoa. It's all right," I said in my most soothing voice. "I just want to get you untangled."

I fished out another carrot, and he drew close once more. While he was distracted by the treat, I managed to gently lift his foot in my hand and work the twine free. "There," I said triumphantly.

It might've been my imagination, but the expression he gave me was something I didn't experience often. Almost as though he could see a deeper part of me than what was on the surface. Like he saw more than an awkwardly tall and fearful girl with the wrong clothes and the wrong eyebrows and the wrong everything else. Like he saw into my heart and liked what he found there.

"You're good with them," a voice broke through the quiet. I whirled around, and the first thing I noticed about the woman was her bold, flower-printed galoshes. She was wearing a floppy sun hat and glasses that hid most of her face, but I could tell by the wrinkly skin on her hands that she was older than my parents by at least a decade or two.

"Um, thanks," I said. "I just stopped because, well . . .

Here." I handed her the now balled-up piece of twine. "I'm on my way home. The Stargazer RV Park?" It came out like a question. Unfortunately, it was.

A warm smile poured onto the woman's face. "Are you lost?"

I cringed at the memory of my Tolkien outburst and the way that boy—Ryan, was it?—used the quote to make fun of me. "Not all those who wander are lost" rang in my head, but I kept my lips sealed and nodded.

"Continue on this road for about a quarter of a mile. Take the first left you come to, then carry on for another mile or so. The RV park will be on your right."

"Thank you," I said. I started to leave, but I couldn't go without one more glance at the animals behind the fence. "They're so fluffy," I said more to myself than the woman.

"That they are," she said. "My name's Rachel. I have a shop in town called Fleece on Earth. I'll be there tomorrow. You should come by."

I nodded. "Maybe," I said. I wanted to stay longer and find out more about her animals and her shop. But I wasn't sure how much time I had before the rest of my family started trickling back to the Gnarly Banana. Carrying Ms. Horton's note was like lugging a bowling ball around in my backpack. Giving it to my parents would be hard enough without first having to explain why I was late coming home.

Luckily, the woman's directions were easy to follow, and I made it to the Gnarly Banana before anyone else arrived. While I waited, I got myself a bowl of cereal for a snack since I'd given away all my carrots. I was smiling to myself, remembering how the sweet animals behind the fence had gingerly taken the carrots from my hand, when my parents walked in.

"Looks like someone had a great first day!" Dad crowed when he saw the look on my face.

"That makes two of us," Mom said. "I got the job at the deli and my wallet is bulging with tips. I think we should celebrate. I bet we can find an ice cream shop after dinner."

"Did someone say ice cream?" Neil crowded in behind my parents. David entered a second later.

"Uh . . ." My mouth hung open. I knew I should tell my parents about the note, maybe even about Cat, and how awful school had been. But there was so much commotion, and my brothers were in surprisingly good moods, and I just couldn't bring myself to do it. I'd suffered enough for one day. The last thing I wanted was to announce my failures when everyone else was finding success. Then Dad's smile would transform into a disappointed frown. Ice cream would be canceled, and my brothers would go back to brooding. Besides, the note didn't say my parents had to contact Ms. Horton immediately. It said at their "earliest convenience." The note could wait.

It took longer to find an open ice cream shop than we thought. We got to bed late and everyone overslept the next morning. We scrambled to get ready, and Dad griped all through breakfast about how hard it was to go back to using an alarm clock.

There definitely wasn't a "convenient" time to bring up Ms. Horton's note before school. We barely made it out the door on time.

Cat's eyes flicked in my direction when I walked into first period. I smiled and her expression softened, but only for a second before frosting over again.

"Here," Mr. Roybal said, and handed me a worksheet. "Grab a laptop and get to work."

I did as he said, thankful there weren't any awkward introductions today. Maybe I could learn to fit in, or at least not be such a spectacle. And I knew I'd slipped up with the library debacle, but if I proved to be a good student, Principal Stinger would have to let me stay.

As soon as I was settled into my seat, I read the first question:

Known as one of America's most famous naturalists and conservationists, this man has also been called "the Father of the National Parks."

I perked up in my seat. I would ace this assignment. No

doubt I'd been to more national parks than anyone else in the class, and my family had the stickers on our trailer to prove it. I even remembered Dad talking about this very man. I couldn't remember his name, but no matter; that's why I had a laptop. Three clicks later I filled in the blank with "John Muir" and moved on to question number two:

In 1872, _____ became the first national park.

I knew this one! Yellowstone—I didn't even need the internet to back me up on it. But the question did get me thinking. I wanted to know when some of the other places I'd visited were given national park status, and what that meant exactly.

Without giving it much thought, I spent the remainder of the class reading online articles about why national parks are important instead of googling and answering the remaining questions on the worksheet.

My parents had always encouraged and rewarded learning that was interest driven. When a topic intrigued me, they gave me all the time I wanted to think about it and research it to my heart's content. They lavished me with praise when I shared information I'd uncovered with the rest of my family.

So, when the bell rang and Mr. Roybal told us to turn in our worksheets on our way out the door, it caught me by surprise. "I . . . I didn't finish," I stammered as I laid my paper on the growing pile atop his desk.

"Two answers," he said in disbelief. "I gave you fifty minutes of work time, and all you came up with was two answers?"

"But—" I wanted to explain myself. He didn't give me the chance.

"You can daydream on your own time. Not in my class-room." Then he wrote an F in red on my paper and drew a circle around it. Apparently, the only thing deep thought would get me in middle school was a bad grade.

I stood there for a minute holding up the line until Cat grabbed my arm. "C'mon," she said. "You're going to make us all late for second period today." The way she said it, though, it wasn't mean or impatient. Just matter-of-fact, if not a little sympathetic.

Despite everything, Cat seemed to be taking her assign-ment as my seventh-grade "ambassador" seriously. She made herself available to answer any questions I had, as long as they were school related. At least, that's what I assumed. The real, true questions simmering in my heart went unasked, and there-fore unanswered.

She was all business when I had to be shown to the school resource center so I could get help with math. It wasn't that I couldn't do the problems. The computer program was confus-ing. I kept entering my answers in the wrong format. Nobody else had trouble, though. They must've all used the program before.

Several times as we'd walked down the hall between classes, Cat opened her mouth like she was going to say something before stopping herself. *Something about my aunt being her mom? Something about the note my family left, or the birthday cards we sent each year? Something about Ryan and how awful he'd treated me? Who knows?*

Finally, on the way to the cafeteria for lunch, I got up the nerve to say, "Did I do something wrong? I mean, I know I've done *a lot* of things wrong since I got here, but you've seemed angry with me from the moment we met."

Cat stopped walking and turned to me. "No," she said. "You didn't do anything." Then she took off and left me standing there to wonder why her answer had sounded so pointed.

I sought her out inside the cafeteria. Maybe if I sat with her and her friends again, I could find a way to slowly bridge the gap between us. But when I saw Ryan at the end of her table, my insides clenched. I redirected myself to a near-empty table on the opposite side of the cafeteria.

There were a few seventh graders at the table where I landed. I noticed they weren't as polished and self-assured as some of the other students. Thinking they might not immediately reject me, I summoned the courage to say hi as I slid close to a girl with a baggy black T-shirt and silver high-top sneakers. She nodded at me and then went back to a conversation she was having with the boy across from her.

I listened in, hoping I could interject something witty or humorous. Something—definitely not a Tolkien quote—to make them pay attention to me, maybe even like me. But I gave up when I realized what they were talking about—gamer tags and Xbox Live memberships. I liked video games and electronics, but my knowledge was pretty much limited to the handheld gaming device my parents had given to me one Christmas. I was way out of my league with these two.

So, I ate my sandwich in silence, and thought about my plans for after school. I wanted to drop by Fleece on Earth—whatever that was—and talk to the woman, Rachel, about her animals. I wanted to ask if it was okay to pet them and feed them carrots.

When I climbed on the bus after school, Cat's eyes skimmed my face. Her expression was unreadable in the few seconds before she shifted her gaze elsewhere.

I wanted to be the type of person who could coolly plop down next to her and confront the issue head-on. Instead, ever the coward, I pretended not to see her and kept walking toward the back of the bus. I wondered if it would go on like this—neither of us talking about the things that should be said—until my family left Winterland. Then we'd be gone from her life again, probably forever. But . . . wouldn't we always be connected in a way because we were related?

Unfortunately, going to find the woman I'd met at the ranch meant getting off the bus at the same stop as the day before. I hung back when the bus rolled into town, this time putting as much space as possible between me and the group Ryan and Cat belonged to. The last thing I wanted was a repeat of yesterday's humiliation.

As I walked, my shorts' pocket bulged with a wad of dollar bills. Mom had given me her remaining tips from the deli after we'd gone for ice cream the night before. I'd bought myself a little extra time today saying I'd use the money to shop for new clothes after school.

When Ryan and Cat's group disappeared into a coffee shop shaped like a train car, I hurried past it and into a round building next door. I thought I could ask for directions to Fleece on Earth. That was, until I saw what waited for me inside.

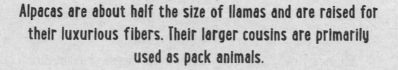

6

Alpacas are about half the size of llamas and are raised for their luxurious fibers. Their larger cousins are primarily used as pack animals.

It was like I'd stepped into a different world—one where Ryan and his snickering friends never existed. A woman stood at a counter. Behind her, a menagerie of wooden animals rose and dipped as they spun around the room. The most delightful music played in the background. It sounded like an entire symphonic band was contained inside the organ at the center of the carousel, with brass instruments and drums beating out notes that were deep and full. They sounded sad yet cheerful.

A man with a gray beard, glasses, and a ponytail sat beside the organ. A cane rested on his knees. He smiled and waved at me, then disappeared as the backside of the organ came into sight. Soft white bulbs illuminated the crested rounding board.

The animals hung on golden poles that extended from cranking rods at the top, down to the platform below. There was music and color and light, and it was all so wonderful. So whimsical. So *magical*.

"Would you like to purchase a ticket?" the woman asked. She had a kind, round face; silver hair; and watchful, sparkling eyes.

My heart beat inside my chest with the most resounding *YES*, but I hesitated. I wanted to find Fleece on Earth. Plus, I didn't have much money for shopping. But I had enough time and money for one ride, didn't I?

"How much?" I asked.

"One dollar."

It seemed a reasonable fare, especially compared to the money my family had shelled out for amusement park rides. I fished a bill out of the pocket in my jean shorts and held it up like a wish.

"Is this your first visit to the Carousel of Wonder?" the woman asked.

I nodded.

"Passing through?"

"No, my family just moved to Winterland," I said, but it didn't sound right since all I'd ever known was "passing through." I reasoned in my head that it was—that living somewhere for several months should count as moving there. And despite my rough first couple of days of school, I still wanted the statement to be true.

"Well, welcome!" she said. "Glad to have you here."

I felt like a first grader again, bubbling with excitement as I deposited the dollar bill in her outstretched hand and she ripped me off a ticket. As I stepped through the passageway and closer to the carousel, the room opened up, taller and rounder. The music grew fuller and louder.

I waited as the animals crept to a stop and the music winded down. Then the man with the ponytail stepped off the platform with the aid of his cane. "Hello there," he said. "My name is Dan, and the young lady out front is Carol."

"My name's Amelia," I said, "Amelia Jean." I handed over my ticket, then peered past him. The eyes on all the animals were so, I don't know . . . soulful. I loved the way many of them seem to be frozen mid-stride—at least until the carousel came to life. Amundsens typically bypassed the carousels at amusement parks for more thrilling rides. But it seemed to me that almost all the carousel animals I'd seen before were horses. I loved the variety of animals on this carousel. I loved everything about it.

"Nice to meet you, Amelia Jean. Now, the Carousel of Wonder is all hand carved," said Dan. "The creator was a soldier. He carried a music box with him on the battlefield. In between firefights, he'd hold the music box up to his ear. The sound brought him peaceful thoughts of a carousel in a mountain meadow. It helped him manage his fears. After he came home from the war, he spent over two decades carving and painting all these colorful creatures you see behind me. Choose any animal you please," he said. "Just watch your feet as you climb on. We don't want to damage them any."

I scurried around the platform from animal to animal. Choosing wasn't easy. There was a lynx, a bear beside a bench, an ostrich, and a rabbit—so many to pick from. Then I saw one that reminded me of the animals I'd met in the field the day before. "Serendipitous," I whispered, and stepped forward.

The animal had its legs drawn together and appeared to be jumping. It wore a saddle on its back and pink ballerina slippers on its feet.

"Fine choice," the man said as I carefully climbed aboard. "The alpaca is my favorite, too."

"Alpaca?" I said. "I thought it was a llama."

He shook his head. "Many people make that mistake. Both are in the camelid family. But if you ask me, the alpaca is a step above its more famous cousin." Before I could ask why, and how one could tell the difference, he added, "Looks like you're the only rider at the moment. Are you ready?"

I nodded and next thing I knew, the circular platform was

moving, and the organ was playing that cheerful yet sad music again, and the alpaca was lifting and falling. Lifting and falling.

Gears cranked overhead. There was so much to see—lights and colors flashed by as I rode around and around. Another carved wooden animal—a racoon, I think—sat on the cranking rod over my alpaca.

I clung to the alpaca's neck. I wished the ride would never end. I wished I could throw my arms around the necks of the real-live alpacas, the way I could this one. I would've ridden the carousel until all my dollars were gone if I didn't so badly want to see those alpacas again. I decided to buy one more ticket, and then ask the woman—Carol, Dan had said her name was—for directions to Fleece on Earth.

The blissful effects of the carousel lasted after it stopped spinning and the golden rods stopped rising and falling. I floated on air off the ride and out to purchase a second ticket. But reality came crashing back when I noticed Cat standing in the lobby.

Carol smiled warmly at me. "Do you know my granddaughter, Cat?" she asked. "The two of you must be around the same age."

"Hi, Amelia," Cat said with a hint of annoyance in her voice.

The woman was Cat's grandmother? The happy buzz evaporated and was immediately replaced by a stomachache.

"Amelia? Amelia Amundsen?" Carol said as recognition dawned on her. "Why, of course. I can't believe I didn't put two and two together when you said your family just moved here."

The air in the room grew impossibly thin and suffocating. None of us seemed to know what to say after that. I wondered if Cat's grandmother resented me, too—if she wished she could take back the welcome she'd extended me minutes before.

As for me, I wished the ground would open up and swallow me whole. Which only made me think of Tolkien. "'In a hole in the ground there lived a hobbit,'" I mumbled. Then, when the look in Carol Winter's eyes changed from surprise to confusion, I blurted, "I should leave now."

"Wait!" Cat's grandmother said, but I already had one foot out the door.

I hurried outside, not paying attention to where I was headed. As soon as the door shut behind me, it was flung open again. "You don't have to go," I heard Cat say. Unfortunately, her tone didn't sound sincere.

I stopped but didn't turn around.

I heard Cat exhale loudly. I didn't know if she'd come after me because she felt like she had to, or because her grandmother told her she must. If I hadn't been through a ton of uncomfortable situations in Winterland already, I might've gone back just to ask her. As it was, I didn't know why things were weird between Cat and me. But they were, and I was sick of feeling gawky and unwanted. I was tired of not knowing what to say, and then saying the wrong thing when I did open my mouth.

If only I'd known my hesitation would make things worse. Because I froze, it gave Ryan time to saunter over from the coffee shop. His eyes flicked to Cat standing inside the doorway, then back to me. "I was wrong about you, Brows," he said in a low, even voice. "Those aren't the thickest eyebrows I've ever seen on a *girl*. They're the thickest eyebrows I've ever seen on a *baby*. Did you have a fun widdle wide on the carousel?"

My cheeks burned and I tried to push past him, but he kept after me. "Great choice, though. I mean, you and that hairy llama have a lot in common."

I hated what he was saying. I hated more that he and I had made the same mistake. *Alpaca*, I corrected him, but only inside my head.

"Will you be wearing ballerina slippers to school tomorrow? Wait, no, that'd be way too classy for you."

How could I have been so stupid? The carousel only made me feel like I'd been transported to a different world. The walls of glass weren't one-way mirrors. It was painful to think about Ryan watching me ride the alpaca (*not* a llama) with a dumb, dreamy expression on my face. I'd been totally oblivious that he was out here laughing at me the entire time.

My eyes stung as I sped across the lot. The market where Dad worked was directly in front of me. I thought about seeking refuge inside, but I didn't want Dad to see me like this. He'd only give me a pep talk about facing my fears and standing up to my tormentors. And I wasn't up for that just now. I really wasn't.

So, I jotted off to the right, around the back of the strip mall, and promptly fell to pieces. I let my hair fall over my face and the tears flow. The thing was, I was tired of nonstop travel, but I didn't know where I fit in in the world now. I was afraid I'd never fit in again. I was afraid I'd always be an outsider.

"I thought that was you. Are you all right, dear?"

I raised my eyes high enough to see flowery galoshes a few feet from where I'd crumbled. I would've recognized those galoshes anywhere.

I sniffled and raised my head.

"Listen, I overheard what that boy said to you. First of all, don't let anyone convince you not to like something that brings light and joy into the world. Second, comparing someone to an alpaca is a compliment of the highest order," she said flatly. "Alpacas are hardy, graceful, gentle, and friendly creatures, not to mention they produce the softest, must luxurious fleece on the planet. That boy is just too dense to know it."

I smiled wanly and nodded.

Rachel extended a hand to help me up from the ground. "Do you have a few minutes? My shop is right around the corner. I think you'll like it."

I sniffled again and she added, "I can also provide a tissue."

Rachel's store was tucked around the back side of the shopping complex. The store's name—Fleece on Earth—was curved around an image of the world. A tiny painted alpaca was situated on top of the blue-and-green globe.

I almost smiled, but the pain was still too fresh.

Rachel flipped over a notice in the window from the side that read BE RIGHT BACK to OPEN.

Inside, there were signs everywhere. They marked colorful garments, handbags, and balls of yarn. They directed customers to PLEASE TOUCH! YOU'LL BE GLAD YOU DID!

I walked over to a bin of scarves and submersed my hand in the softness. "Oh," I said. "Like reaching into clouds." Then I felt silly again. That was probably something a toddler would say. Not a seventh grader.

The skin around Rachel's eyes crinkled as her face lit brightly. "Isn't it, though?" she said. "You could say I was inspired by Sugar Plum to start the ranch and open this store."

"Sugar Plum?" I asked, confused.

"The carousel's alpaca; she's named after the sugar plum fairy from the *Nutcracker* ballet."

"Oh, of course," I said. But "Attend a Ballet Performance" had never been jotted down on any of the slips in the Amundsen Adventure Jar.

Rachel retrieved a tissue from a box near the checkout register. She placed it in my hand. I took the tissue from her, even though my tears had already dried. "Thank you," I said. I didn't want to talk about my most recent humiliation. Besides, I was far more interested in hearing about her ranch. "The animals I saw yesterday, they were alpacas. Do you have more of them, more than the ones I saw, I mean?"

"I do!" Rachel beamed. "In fact, I have an entire herd of them. When they're sheared, I send some of their fiber to co-ops to be made into the different products I sell here in the shop. My family and I wash, dye, and spin the rest of the fiber at the ranch," she said proudly. She paused to soak in my reaction, then she added, "I was thinking, maybe you'd like a job?"

"What?" Had I heard her correctly?

"It's part-time, of course. A few hours here and there, mostly on the weekends. It doesn't pay much, and it won't be easy. I need someone to help with repairs, and general care of the alpacas. You won them over so easily yesterday. They don't respond that way to everyone."

My emotions were all over the place. After having been so low, I bounced back with too much enthusiasm. "I—I would love to work on your ranch! Yes, please," I said. It was only after I accepted that I realized I should've told her I needed to ask my parents first.

Rachel didn't seem to mind my overeagerness. She reached behind the register again and produced a business card. "Come by on Saturday," she said.

"Thank you. I will." I took the card and was about to leave, when I was struck with an idea. "Um, how much are the scarves?" I asked as I dug out all the bills I had left in my pocket.

Rachel considered for a moment. "How much money do you have there?"

I unwadded the roll and, one by one, laid dollar bills on the counter. After riding the carousel, I had fourteen dollars left. Maybe it would've been enough to buy a new pair of pants, maybe not. But I figured I could make do with the ones I had. I wasn't sure I could go on living without one of the featherlight scarves.

"You're in luck," Rachel said. "That's precisely what they cost."

I picked the prettiest one out of the bin, one with shades of green, gold, orange, and purple, and wrapped it around my neck. It felt *incredible*—like wearing a hug. But I was smart enough to know that things in stores were rarely sold in even dollar amounts. Not after taxes were added, anyway. "Are you sure fourteen dollars is enough?"

"Fourteen dollars," Rachel said again, "that is, with your employee discount."

7

Alpacas were revered by ancient Incas, who segregated
them into herds and bred them by color. Thanks to the
Incas, alpacas now produce twenty-two
distinguishable fleece colors.

Mom wasn't angry exactly, but I could tell she was a little
miffed about the way I'd spent her tips from the deli.
"So much for being smarter about how we use our
money," she grumbled. When she saw the crushed expression
on my face, she added, "It's a beautiful scarf, Amelia Jean. I can
see why you wanted it. You don't have many pretty things. I
just . . . It's *August*. It's *really* hot. A scarf wasn't the most practical choice."

"We're not the most practical family, though, are we?" Dad
said. His eyes met mine in the rearview mirror. He winked, but
I could tell the workday had taken its toll on him. The creases in
his forehead were deeper than usual. I'd met up with my parents
at the market after my "shopping excursion." They were giving

me a ride home, even though I would've preferred to walk so I could visit the alpacas again.

Mom exhaled loudly, and there was amusement in her voice when she said, "I guess we're not." She started to swivel back around in her seat, and then stopped herself. "Oh! Have you bumped into Catherine at school yet?"

"Um, uh-huh," I said.

"And?" Dad asked. I could see in the rearview mirror that his eyes were on me again instead of on the road.

I squirmed a little. "She's nice," I said truthfully, because I could tell she was a nice person. She just wasn't all that nice to me.

After waiting a few beats, Dad asked. "That's it? That's all you have to say?"

"Yeah, I mean, I don't really know her yet," I said, which was also true.

Dad's eyes flicked to mine yet again, and I could see he was growing frustrated with me for not sharing more. What did he want? Was I supposed to somehow mend the family by befriending his niece? I thought he'd wanted me to meet my cousin for my benefit, not his.

I could feel the muscles in my jaw tighten.

This time Mom defused the situation. She finally did swivel all the way forward, and then she placed a hand on Dad's arm.

"Let Amelia be. Seems like it's been a long second day for all of us. Guess the honeymoon phase is over already." She laughed hollowly.

After that, Dad's eyes stayed on the road. I was thankful I didn't have to explain how Cat seemed to be holding a grudge against me. Or reveal that I was being treated far worse by Ryan.

Then there was the job offer . . . *One revelation at a time*, I told myself. *I'll tell my parents about the alpacas later . . . maybe after dinner?* A sickening thought hit me that I still had to give them Ms. Horton's letter, too. *Definitely after dinner, then.* Dad was always more relaxed when his belly was full.

It seemed like a good plan—waiting for the right moment to spring all my news on them—but that was before I saw what was waiting for us back at the Gnarly Banana. When we rolled into the Stargazer RV Park, Neil and David were hunched down in front of the yellow travel trailer. It wasn't until Mom, Dad, and I hopped out of the truck that we could see what my brothers were so interested in.

A dog lapped water from one of our cereal bowls. Her sides were rippled by her protruding rib cage. She was as red as a Utah sunrise. She had pointy ears, and clumps of dried mud hung from her tail and the fur on her legs.

"She was wandering around the RV park," Neil explained, "panting like crazy."

"She was frightened at first," David chimed in. "She cowered and walked wide circles around us when we tried to get close. But she warmed up quickly when we gave her some water." He gently patted the dog on her back. "Can we get her some food, too?"

I turned to Dad, but for some reason his face was clenched while everyone else was smiling. Mom glanced from David to my father and back to David. The expression on her face grew as somber as Dad's. "You know we can't have pets," she said with a sigh.

This wasn't the first time the topic had been raised. David had brought in a stray cat once, a few years ago, and named him Oscar. Oscar traveled across six states with us. But he escaped one day while the Gnarly Banana was parked at a rest stop in Idaho. We waited hours for him to return, until our parents said we couldn't wait any longer. David cried for days.

Obviously, my parents thought we were wandering into dangerous, heartbreaking territory again by feeding a vagrant dog. Pets and the Amundsen lifestyle didn't mix well.

"I know," David said, his voice laden with disappointment. "It's just temporary. You know, until we can find her a good home."

It's just temporary—that pretty much sums up our entire existence, I thought.

The dog chose that moment to lick my father's hand, and

Dad huffed. He fought to keep the corners of his mouth from rising and lost the battle. "Well, I suppose we can't let her starve," he said. "I need to head back to town to do a load of laundry anyway. I'll pick up some chow while I'm there. But, listen, don't let her in the trailer, and don't give her a name, okay?" He groaned. "It'll just make things harder on everybody when we have to give her up."

. . .

"I'm calling her Annie," David whispered in my ear, "like the orphan. What do think?" We were seated at the table, aka my bed. I was completing a social studies assignment, and he was focusing on geometry homework. He'd worked some of the mud clots out of the dog's fur, fed her, and she was curled up on a floor mat outside the trailer.

I thought Annie was a perfect name for a dog as red as a Utah sunrise, but I bit my lip and shrugged. "It's okay, I guess . . ." What if Dad's reaction to my new job was the same as it had been to the stray dog? The offer to work with Rachel's alpacas was the best thing that had happened to me in months. I'd be devastated if my parents said no. I was also worried if I brought up the meeting with Principal Stinger, they'd be so upset they wouldn't say yes to anything for a long time. Telling them about the job had to come first.

I pulled Rachel's business card from my pocket and nervously flicked the top right-hand corner with my index finger. With the extra stop for dog food, Dad was late getting back, and dinner had been rushed. Then our furry red visitor had commanded everyone's attention as she gobbled down chow. Also, petting her as she lavished us with sloppy dog kisses had been essential. There hadn't been a good time to tell my parents about the ranch . . . until now.

I cleared my throat and was about to open my mouth when Neil beat me to it. "Did you know there are fifty-three fourteeners in Colorado?" he said.

Dad let out a low whistle as he handed a clean dish to Mom to stack in the cupboard next to the sink.

Neil swung away from the computer to face the rest of us. "Don't you think it'd be pity, a missed opportunity even, if we didn't summit at least one of the fourteeners while we were here?"

David perked up. "I've always wanted to climb a fourteener."

The skin on the back of my neck rose with tiny goose pimples. "What is a fourteener?" I asked, dreading the answer.

"That's a great idea!" Dad said, ignoring my question as he rushed to join Neil at the computer. He seemed more animated than I'd seen him since we'd arrived in Winterland.

"But we'll have to get acclimated first. We should start with some easier hikes. We can work our way up. I can't believe we didn't think of this sooner—a bonus challenge will get everyone in shape for skiing the black diamond."

While Neil and Dad started making plans for a warm-up hike on Saturday, David turned to me. "To be a fourteener, a mountain peak has to rise at least fourteen thousand feet above sea level."

My breath hitched in my throat.

"Climbing one is tough," David said. "Strenuous activity, you know. Plus, at that altitude, the air is thin, and there's a ton of exposure to heights. It sounds *awesome*."

Heights? "I'm not going," I blurted loudly.

Mom shut off the sink faucet. Dad turned to look at me and frowned. Adventures had always been a family affair. I'd always gone along with them, never really putting up a protest. But I'd never had any other options before. This time I did. I showed them the card Rachel had given me. "I . . . I have my own plans," I stammered. "I got a job—working at an alpaca ranch."

"You can't have a job," Neil said. "You're a kid. People don't hire kids."

"Yes, they can," I shot back. At the same time a flicker of doubt entered my mind.

"You're just jealous," David said, coming to my defense. "Just because you've never been gainfully employed doesn't mean Amelia can't be."

"Why would you want a job?" Dad asked, like the notion was unfathomable.

Mom took the card from me and studied it. "The ranch is right down the road," she said. "You could easily walk there."

I nodded.

Mom and Dad exchanged a look that made me wonder if they'd been expecting this day to come. Like, maybe they'd suspected all along that I wasn't as big of an adrenaline junkie as the rest of them and would one day find a way to worm out of family adventures.

"Spill the details," Mom said.

So, I told her all about Rachel and Fleece on Earth, and I let her assume that I'd wandered into the store looking for new clothes instead of a tissue because I'd been crying my eyes out.

"I'm not sure I'm comfortable with this, Amelia Jean . . . Working? At your age?" Dad said dubiously.

"Why do you have to say no to everything?" David grumbled.

"What that's supposed to mean?" Dad asked.

"I think he means the dog," I said.

Dad sighed heavily. Then, while I had him on the defense, I drove in the nail with one of his favorite Tolkien quotes. "'All we have to decide is what to do with the time that is given us,' right? *This* is what I want to do with the time given to me. I want to spend Saturday working with alpacas, not going on some ridiculously hard hike just to get ready for an even harder one."

Dad looked on the verge of blowing a gasket.

"I think," Mom said calmly, "that a compromise can be reached. I'll contact this Rachel, and if everything checks out, Amelia Jean can work there as long as it doesn't interfere with her schoolwork."

"Or our family adventures," Dad added. "Amelia, you need to be going on these hikes even more than the rest of us . . ."

My skin prickled. Why? Because I was the weakest physically or because I still hadn't conquered my fear of heights? Either felt like a slap to the face.

"I'll make an exception for this Saturday, since you've already given your word," Dad continued. "But after that, school and family come first. If you don't have enough time for all three, you know which one has to go."

I nodded, because what other choice did I have?

"You'll have plenty of years to work when you're older," Dad said. "I think after a taste of it, you'll change your mind about how you want to spend your time."

Apparently, Rachel made a good impression on my mom (which wasn't a surprise), because when I got home from school the next day, my parents didn't go back on our agreement. They made me promise to behave, and not get in the way. They didn't ask any questions about the incident outside the carousel, or the mean boy who'd teased me to the point of tears. So I knew Rachel hadn't ratted me out, and that made me like her even more.

Still, I felt like I was on shaky ground. I didn't want to give my parents any reason to doubt that I could handle school and a job. Like, maybe it wasn't a good idea to bring up that I'd been carrying around a note from school for a few days because I'd gotten off to a rocky start. Not until I could prove to my parents that I had everything under control. The thing was, the longer I kept it a secret and nothing happened, the easier it was to think the problem might just go away on its own.

Unfortunately, it didn't. At the end of the school day on Friday, my last-period teacher handed me another note from Ms. Horton about scheduling a meeting with the principal. All my panic came flooding back. *I have to tell them*, I thought. *I have to give Ms. Horton's notes to my parents.* But it was *so* close to being Saturday. An image of the adorable alpacas sprang to mind—I couldn't do anything to jeopardize seeing them the next day. *Besides*, I reasoned, *the school office will be closed over the weekend*. My parents couldn't reach Ms. Horton if they tried. I crumpled the letter and crammed it in the same pocket of my backpack as the first.

I'd worn my colorful new scarf and it had garnered me a few

looks—it really wasn't scarf weather, but I didn't care. And it didn't escape Ryan's attention on the bus ride home. "Do us all a favor, Brows," he said, "and wrap that thing a little higher, so it'll cover your ugly face." He'd probably been working on the insult all day and couldn't wait until we got off the bus to sling it at me.

Cat and another girl were seated in a row diagonal from mine. The second girl, whose name I didn't know, smiled at me pityingly. "My aunt says if a boy is mean to you, it's because he likes you," she said.

I knew she meant well, but I also knew that wasn't true. It was something adults said to make you feel better. I smiled back weakly and turned to face the window.

"That's stupid," I heard Cat say to the other girl. "If you like someone, you should never intentionally be mean to them. End of story."

I had an urge to thank Cat. To say something to her, anything. But I quickly squashed that idea. By now, I knew my way around the school. Her services as an "ambassador" were no longer needed. Plus, things had been even weirder between us since the incident outside the carousel. I mean, she did follow me out the door, but it wasn't like she hadn't made her feelings clear before then. She didn't want me to be a part of her life in Winterland. She didn't want me to be a part of her life at all.

8

During the 1500s, Spanish conquistadors slaughtered millions of alpacas with the intent to devastate and control the Incan Empire. The native people who survived took refuge in remote areas of the Andes Mountains with the remnants of their alpaca herds.

Even though I *could've* easily walked to the ranch, my parents insisted on driving me there on the way to their hike. Mom wanted to meet Rachel before leaving me under her supervision. She was fidgety in the front seat of the cab—adjusting the AC and turning down the music. I realized she was nervous. My parents had hardly ever left me in someone else's care. Here I was a middle schooler—one who had been in countless dangerous situations, which she and Dad had led me into, no less—and she was worried about leaving me with an elderly woman and her sweet, furry animals? No wonder I'd never fit in with my peers.

"This is it," Dad said after less than two minutes behind the wheel. He pulled the cab off the main road onto a long dirt drive. Rachel's herd was behind a fence off to the right. They raised their fuzzy heads in interest, and Dad stopped the truck while I rolled down the cab window to get a better look.

The alpacas came in an array of colors—white, tan, brown, gray, and black. Some were puffy as cotton balls; others had long silky locks. Their eyes looked disproportionately large for their heads—that is, the eyes I could see. Some of the alpacas had floppy bangs hiding everything on their faces except their protruding noses. Every single one was adorable, in a decidedly awkward way. I picked out the creamy white one from the rest, the one who'd taken the carrot from my hand. I couldn't wait to meet the others.

We continued down the drive for a bit until we found Rachel standing on the wraparound porch of a quaint mountain home. The house was made of wood and stone and had pointed dormer windows. Sunflowers and wild grasses sprouted along either side of the road. A large barn sat catty-corner from the main house. Around it, there were a number of small pastures, and a maze of fences and gates and small three-sided structures.

"'Still round the corner there may wait. A new road or a secret gate,'" I said. I met Dad's gaze in the rearview mirror. The lines around his eyes crinkled as I quoted Tolkien. I smiled back at him.

It all seemed so inviting. Even Mom sighed when she saw the little greenhouse near the side of the structure. This was more than a place where people lived. It was a home. A place where a family nurtured plants and animals and, over time, built a life together. The Gnarly Banana came close, and I'd heard the saying "Home is where the heart is" hundreds of times. No doubt, my heart was with my family—even if that meant it was on wheels. But lately, I'd been longing for something else. Something more.

The entire Amundsen family filed out of the truck, except Annie (aka the nameless dog), who remained in the back seat. David had somehow convinced my parents to let him bring her along.

My brothers acted like they were only interested in heart-pulsing action. But I think a quieter life called to them, too, now and then. Neil's eyes scanned the ranch. His gaze landed on a window looking into Rachel's kitchen. There was a large granite island, stainless steel appliances, and a breakfast nook. The ample-sized eating area was flooded with natural light. He raised an eyebrow, then looked at me and nodded in approval. "Almost makes me want to skip the hike, too," he said. "*Almost.*"

It was the open fields that drew a look of longing from David.

Rachel and my parents exchanged pleasantries. Mom reminded me for the billionth time not to be a nuisance—which seemed very unprofessional and made me blush, because I was here to work, which is the opposite of being a nuisance. Then my family loaded back up. Rachel and I stood on the gravel drive and watched them leave.

"Well." Rachel's eyes flicked to the scarf around my neck, then back to my face, and she smiled warmly. "Why don't we meet the alpacas first?"

Don't get me wrong, I adored Sugar Plum, the carousel alpaca. But real-live fluffy and silly alpacas were on a whole 'nother level. As she led me through a hinged gate leading to a small pasture, Rachel said I should approach the alpacas slowly and calmly and use a soothing voice when speaking to them. "Some are a little skittish, but most of mine enjoy being petted gently on the neck or back," she explained.

She introduced me to Ed first. Ed's trunk and legs were gray, and he had a white stripe running up his chest and neck. He jut ted his bottom teeth out at me—his *only* teeth. I hadn't noticed it before, but apparently alpacas don't have any incisors along the front of their upper jaws. Just smooth pink gums.

Rachel told me to open my hand, and then she dumped an apple cut in small, bite-sized pieces into it. Ed took the first slice, brushing and tickling my palm with his fuzzy lips, and rolled the morsel around with his tongue. He then attempted to pul-verize the piece by smashing it against the roof of his mouth. A little apple juice came squirting out, and I took a step back.

Rachel laughed. "Alpacas are very efficient at eating grass, but apples not so much."

Ed happily worked his jaw side to side, and occasionally his lips smacked together. He'd hardly finished the first bite before he was sniffing around for more. He greedily snagged the next one from my hands, and I got another look at the long teeth poking out of his bottom jaw.

"Ed is due for a trim," Rachel said.

"His teeth?" I asked.

"Yes, they'll keep growing and growing until they extend over his upper jaw. He'll become very uncomfortable unless we get them grinded down soon. I'll put it on the to-do list for this weekend."

I watched her carefully. Did she want *me* to take part in grinding Ed's teeth? Going to the dentist made me squirm. How would I ever inflict that kind of discomfort on another living thing?

But Rachel seemed too distracted by her thoughts for me to clarify her intentions. When her gaze returned from somewhere off in the distance, she said, "I'm afraid I haven't been able to stay on top of things like teeth trimming since my husband passed away. My son and his wife help all they can. My daughter-in-law, Julie, is running the shop today. And Heath, my son, is delivering orders for our composted alpaca manure. But the ranch operations are more than the three of us can handle without Harold."

I shifted my weight around on my feet the same way Ed rolled the apple with his tongue. "I'm sorry," I said, and I was, in more ways than one. I was sorry for her loss, and also because I hadn't known until then that this job came with a void larger than anything I could ever fill.

Rachel patted my hand. "I shouldn't concern you with my problems. Let's go see some of the others, shall we?"

We continued walking through the field. She introduced me to Lulu next. Lulu was puffy, soft, and white all over, except for her eyelashes, which were black as night. She tipped her head to one side and batted her long lashes as if to say, *Am I not the cutest thing you've ever seen?*

And she was, she truly was—like a cartoon animal, with eyes drawn overly large and expressive. I took one look at her and couldn't help but give her the choicest apple slice I had left in my hand. Unlike Ed, she munched it daintily, and not a single drop of apple juice escaped her lips.

"I know," Rachel said, reading the expression on my face. "And I swear she does, too. Lulu is our resident diva."

Something gently bumped me from behind, and I turned to find an alpaca the color of golden wheat sidling up to me. His fur hung long, and it was shiny and almost curtain-like instead of being all fluffed out like a teddy bear.

"That's Benny. He's a suri alpaca. They're not as common as the huacaya"—she said this like *wa-Ki-ya*—"but they both come from South America. The huacaya fleece is good for making things like socks, mittens, sweaters, and scarves—like the one you're wearing. Suri fibers have more luster and are better for outerwear—like coats and shawls. Both are softer than sheep's wool, water-resistant, and hypoallergenic."

The wheat-colored alpaca nudged me again, and Rachel added, "Benny's a real charmer, but watch out for Carl—the two of them are inseparable. While Benny is distracting you with snuggles, Carl will sneak off with your hat or water bottle."

Sure enough, a lighter-colored suri alpaca was teasing the last apple slice from my fingers. I hadn't even noticed. I opened my hand and let him take it.

"What about llamas?" I asked, thinking of Dan's comment that alpacas were, in his opinion, superior to their more famous cousins. "Do you have any here on the ranch? Do they have soft fleece, too?"

"Well, llama fleece is typically coarser and not as consistent. It doesn't come in as many color variations as alpaca fleece—alpacas come in twenty-two different shades, and their fibers dye beautifully. Llamas are about twice the size of alpacas, and their ears are longer, more banana-shaped," Rachel said. "While alpacas have been bred for their soft fiber, llamas have been bred for their strength. They're used more as a pack animal. You know, to carry heavy things around for us humans. Oh, and they also make good guard animals. I don't have any here on the ranch, but I've been thinking about adding some, along with goats, to keep the sagebrush down and mitigate fire danger. But, the more we expand, the more labor that's required and . . ."

Rachel started to look sad and distant again, but then she came back to me. "Anyway, enough about llamas and goats. Let's go visit the cria, shall we?"

"Cria?" I repeated.

"You'll see," Rachel said. Her hazel eyes twinkled in the warm morning sunlight. And I liked the way her short hair appeared even more silvery outdoors.

We passed by other alpacas in other pastures, but we didn't stop. Instead, Rachel led me to a pen closest to the barn. As I neared the fence, a baby alpaca stared up at me inquisitively. His fur was a rich, dark brown with a hint of red. The tip of his nose and his ears were black. He hummed softly.

I thought my heart might explode.

"Meet the newest member of our ranch. This is Samson." Rachel gestured at the attentive little creature behind the fence, then at the docile adult alpaca behind him. "His mother's name is Hazel."

As if on cue, Samson arched his back and sprang into the air. He did this repeatedly, bouncing around the pen as well as his mother, who happened to be a lighter shade of brown. He reminded me of Sugar Plum, lifting and dropping on the carousel pole.

I giggled, watching him entertain himself with all that leaping about. "So, baby alpacas are called 'crias'?"

"That's right," Rachel said.

I bounced my head along with Samson's movements. When I reached my hand out to touch him the way Rachel had shown me, he startled and sprang away.

"Did I mention that most alpacas are timid creatures?" Rachel asked, almost consolingly. "They're afraid of their own shadows. But the more you're around them, the more they'll trust you."

While Rachel was talking, Samson sniffed at a harmless insect crawling in the dirt. The insect fluttered away suddenly, and Samson again jolted with fear. Rachel chuckled softly. "See," she said.

I felt an instant bond with the easily frightened baby alpaca. "Do you have very many of them?" I asked hopefully. "Crias, I mean."

"Just the one. Although . . . next weekend we'll find out if we have another one on the way," Rachel said cryptically. "Now, I would love to watch Samson pronk around all day, but I'm afraid there's work to be done. Are you okay with lifting hay bales?"

"Sure," I said. I never felt strong when I was around my family, but maybe I hadn't been given the right task. Also, lifting hay bales sounded better than grinding teeth.

"Great," she said. "Come with me, we'll use the cart."

I helped Rachel load a wheelbarrow with two bales of hay and we bump, bump, bumped it along the uneven ground out to a hay feeder in one of the pastures. She loaned me a pair of work gloves. The straws scratched at the exposed skin of my forearms anyway. They looked like I'd been caught in catfight after we transferred the bales to the feeder.

I also learned why Rachel wore galoshes all the time. The pastures were a minefield of puddles, but the rubbery galoshes provided her protection against more than mud. Prickly plants pierced the bare skin around my ankles—the parts that my too-short pants didn't cover.

It wasn't long before my arms ached from transferring bales from the stack in the barn to the cart, and from the cart to the feeder. It was hard work and my body protested. But the weird thing was, I didn't care. The more beat up and exhausted I grew, the stronger I felt. My entire life, any time my family faced something difficult, I'd been a hindrance to everyone around me. Without fail, when we had to stop and rest or were forced to quit an activity, it had been my fault. I was too slow, too weak, or too scared.

That wasn't happening here. Not today. I wasn't a nuisance or a hindrance. My height didn't make me awkward. It helped me reach higher bales. My long legs and arms didn't make me clumsy. They made me more capable of getting the job done.

Dad was wrong. I liked working. It made me feel useful for once.

After countless trips back and forth between the barn and the hay feeders scattered around the ranch, Rachel pointed out how the fence surrounding Samson and Hazel's pen needed repair. Old wooden boards were starting to rot. They would have to be torn out and replaced with new ones.

"I'd like you to help with things done regularly—like feeding the alpacas—and with other, larger projects. This fence is the most pressing item beyond the day-to-day operations of the ranch. Is the repair something you think you can help me tackle?" Rachel asked. "I'll get the supplies, of course, but it'll take a lot of hacking and sawing, not to mention hammering and staining the new posts . . . and out in this heat." She wiped sweat from her forehead with a glove. "Unfortunately, winter will be too cold, and it can't be put off until spring. It needs to be addressed now before it becomes a problem."

I studied the rotting posts. Almost the entire fence would need to be replaced. I wasn't a carpenter or a handyman. I'd rarely swung a hammer. The job felt too big. It was too much. Rachel had been so kind to me. I didn't want to let her down, but this had the whiff of something I would surely fail at.

Rachel must've sensed my hesitation because she said, "You've been a terrific help today, but I need someone who is willing to see this project through. I can pay you for the work you've done, and you can walk away if that's what you want. But if you're willing to put in the effort—it won't be easy—I think you can handle it."

"I . . . I don't know how to build a fence," I stammered.

"Of course not. I didn't expect that you would. I'll teach you. You'll learn. That's not the issue. The issue is whether you're willing to try."

I paused to consider, and then slowly nodded. Of all the things I was afraid of, hard work was not one of them.

Rachel smiled. "Good. Now let's go find a shady tree. I could use a rest." We wound our way down a path to a grassy spot at the edge of a lake on the far end of her property. It was cooler in the shade, but not by much.

"The waterline is so low," Rachel commented. "It's this dry August heat."

August, I thought. The first snowstorm and the completion of my family's Ski a Black Diamond Challenge would be months away. I had plenty of time to repair a fence while I spent the hours blissfully surrounded by alpacas.

Then I could visit the alpacas and the ranch in my mind after we moved away. I thought of the soldier who'd carved the carousel and the way his music box made him think of a carousel in a meadow and how it calmed him on the battlefield. Maybe we all needed a place we could tether our daydreams to.

I snuck a glance at Rachel. She was smiling wistfully and staring out over the serene lake. "So, tell me about yourself," she said, turning her gaze to meet mine. "Your mother said you're staying at the Stargazer RV Park and that you do quite a bit of traveling. That must be exciting."

"I guess," I said. I didn't like talking about myself—it made me feel uncomfortable because I never knew the right thing to say.

"What's been you're favorite destination?"

I almost said Winterland. There was something wonderful about the way mountain peaks all around made me feel. I knew there were dangerous, frightening things in the woods— mountain lions, bears, Lyme-disease-infested ticks, not to mention rocky precipices. But somehow, I felt safe here. Like maybe the craggy peaks were gentle giants standing guard over all the alpine inhabitants. However, Rachel was one of the only people I'd met in Winterland who, as far as I knew, didn't think I was an oddball. I didn't want to say anything weird and change her mind.

So, instead, I said, "I don't know, maybe the redwoods?" And it sounded like a question—which was silly. I was supposed to be answering her question. "Northern California," I said more convincingly.

It really was amazing, all the different places I'd been. I'd seen trees that grew to dizzying heights, and skyscrapers that reached even higher. I'd seen soft ocean waves ebb and flow across sandy beaches, as well as places where the ocean met land with more, I don't know . . . vigor? Places where the surf clashed with the rocky shorelines and water was sprayed high into the air. I'd seen red cliffs, and gray ones, and I'd crawled through cavernous spaces inside a mountain's belly.

The Adventure Jar had taken us Amundsens to some incredible places. And I was thankful for all of it. But . . . all along, there had been a want deep inside me. A want for a center, a base or foundation . . . I wasn't sure how to describe it. What I did know was that the want seemed to be growing larger by the day.

9

Although alpaca fleece had been utilized and valued by the Incas for centuries, it wasn't until the mid-1800s that Europeans began to appreciate its potential for soft yarns and garment making.

Since Rachel hadn't purchased any of the materials for the fence yet, I spent the afternoon sweeping out the barn and meeting the rest of the herd. I was finally introduced to one of the alpacas I'd met that first day, the one who'd had a piece of twine wrapped around his leg. His name was Chai Latte. Rachel said her daughter-in-law named him after her favorite drink.

I felt like I could hang out with him and Ed and Lulu and even Carl all day and listen to the soft humming sounds they made to communicate with one another.

Mom must've worried about me the whole time they were gone, though, because my parents showed up an hour earlier than expected. Or maybe my family was that much faster at hiking up a trail when I wasn't there to slow them down. Either way, I wasn't ready to leave when the truck came rambling down Rachel's long dirt drive.

"Thank you so much for letting me work on your ranch, Ms. Rachel. I had an *amazing* time," I said.

"You are most welcome," Rachel replied, her eyes shining back at me with warmth and generosity.

My brothers were near the back of the truck, letting Annie lap water from a cup. Dad came around from the driver's side, while Mom was sitting in the passenger seat with the window rolled down.

"Yes, we hope Amelia wasn't too much trouble," Dad said. His comment made my ears burn. Why did he assume I'd been a bother? Because I was to the rest of my family?

"Nonsense. I appreciated having the extra pair of hands. Honestly, having Amelia around lightened my load a great deal," Rachel said.

When she turned to me, I tried to convey my gratitude with a smile. Her nose crinkled with delight and she said, "I'll work on gathering supplies the next few days, okay? Come visit me at Fleece on Earth later this week. I'll pay you for the work you did today, and we can figure out a schedule."

I thanked her once more, and then scrambled into the cab along with my brothers and Annie. As we drove away, I gazed out the window at Rachel's herd of alpacas. A sense of loss pinged in my stomach. I missed them already.

. . .

First thing Sunday morning, Dad made my brothers and me print FOUND DOG posters. Although Annie still hadn't been let inside the trailer, we kept feeding her and she persisted in hanging around.

One corner of the Gnarly Banana was set up as our "home office," with the laptop we sometimes used for online classes, a printer, and a mobile router for Wi-Fi.

David took the worst possible photo of Annie. It was blurry, taken from behind, and her head was down, half buried in sagebrush. I didn't see how anyone could recognize her from it. But maybe that was the point.

Dad peered over Neil's shoulder at the computer screen, while my oldest brother put the finishing touches on the poster. "You have the last digit of your mother's cell phone number wrong," Dad said. He sounded annoyed.

"Oops, do I?" Neil said. "My bad." He corrected what we all knew had been an intentional mistake and then clicked print.

Dad dropped David, Neil, Annie, and me off in the center of town. After we hopped out, he rolled down his window. "I'll meet you by the market in an hour," he said. "I don't want you getting back in the truck with any of those posters still in your possession."

David grinned mischievously; a long, dark eyebrow curled upward.

"Don't even think about it," Dad groaned. "You actually need to hang them. Don't you dare throw them away," he said as he pulled away from the curb.

I started our assignment by taping the first one to the center of a nearby light pole. David said, "Here, let me help you with that." He removed the poster and repositioned it low to the ground on the back side, where unless you were two feet tall, you'd have to bend down to read it. "There. Much better," he said, and grinned at me.

He had Annie on a leash he'd fashioned from a rope. She looked up at me and wagged her tail. I scratched behind her ears. All traces of mud were gone. Now that my brothers had bathed her, her fur was soft and clean. She wasn't alpaca fluffy, but she was close.

We spent the next forty-five minutes tacking up posters in the most unlikely-to-be-seen places: on the rear side of dumpsters, the underside of benches, and in the darkest corners of the most desolate streets—not that there were many dark alleys in the small town of Winterland.

We arrived back in the center of town empty-handed and

with fifteen minutes to spare. With nothing better to do until Dad returned, I found myself wandering toward the Carousel of Wonder. My brothers and Annie trailed behind as I approached the round building with tall glass windows. The carved wooden animals were spinning inside—around and around in a blur. Children's faces were full of light and laughter as they passed by. More than half the riders were adults, and their joy was just as obvious.

I cocked my head as I watched the happiness being spun right before my eyes. It truly was a magical place. Then a single face inside the building came into focus. Cat was peering straight at me through the glass. Straight through me, was more like it.

Neil stepped up behind me. "Who's that?" he asked.

"Cat," I said. "I mean, Catherine Winter. Our cousin." She hadn't come up since I'd told my parents she was "nice" and nothing more. Mom must've suspected it was a sensitive topic, because my parents had left me alone about it.

"Why didn't you say so?" Neil said. "Let's go meet her."

"Neil, wait!" I called, but he and David were bounding away like gazelles before I could stop them. By the time I caught up, they had Annie tied to a post outside and Cat cornered inside the building. I hung back only a foot or two inside the entrance and observed. I expected Cat to give them the same frosty treatment I'd received, and I didn't want to get caught in it again.

She was stiff *at first*. But then, as she answered their questions with replies I couldn't hear, her whole demeanor changed. She relaxed, even laughed at something Neil said. I crept forward until their voices were audible.

"That's awesome!" my oldest brother barked. He punched David's arm lightly. "Dude, I love that we have a cousin with serious slope skills." Then he clasped his hands together in front of Cat and begged, "You HAVE to teach us."

"We'll see," Cat said, but she didn't sound totally opposed to it.

What just happened? I was mystified and more than a little annoyed. I'd spent an entire week at school with our cousin and she hadn't cracked a single smile for me. My brothers had spent all of two minutes with her and she was already agreeing to, what? Coach them on the ski slopes? If only I could be half as disarming as my brothers.

I took another step closer. But my irritation only grew as my brothers continued to fawn all over her. I could tell they were impressed when she started talking about freestyle races and ski jumps, and I thought, *They've never once been that impressed by anything I've done.* But Cat was different than I was. She was brave, and apparently, she was an athlete, too.

The realization caused my heart to plummet into my

stomach because I knew . . . I knew they'd much rather have someone like Cat for a sister than someone like me.

Later that evening, when my brothers animatedly told my parents about the encounter, I felt jealous all over again. But for a different reason. Hearing about Cat and my brothers bonding made my parents happy. And it was just one more way that they'd been able to please them where I had failed.

After everyone else had gone to bed, I took the Adventure Jar down from the cupboard and read the slips. I told myself I wasn't being sneaky. My parents would've let me peek at the slips anyway, if I'd asked. Probably. Except I didn't want them looking at my face while I read them. I wasn't sure I could fake excitement that long. One slip at a time was easy. But slip after slip of hair-raising activities? *Oof.* I guess I was hoping to find something in the jar that I might excel at. Something I'd be able to do down the road that would make my parents proud.

But I only made it through a handful of slips before dread got the better of me and I couldn't read anymore. Ride a zip line in the Catskills Camp in an underground cave in Tennessee. Go storm chasing in Tornado Alley. The thought of the things that would thrill them gave me shivers up my spine. I'd swear I was adopted if I didn't look so much like my brothers.

Despite the rough time I was having at school and my inability to win over Cat the way my brothers had, I got a sick feeling when I thought about packing up and leaving again. We'd only been in Winterland for a little over a week, but thanks to the carousel and Rachel's ranch, I already felt more rooted here than anywhere else we'd stopped in the past five years.

So many thoughts and mixed-up emotions were churning inside me as I returned the jar, climbed into bed, and eventually fell asleep. My brain picked up right where it had left off when I awoke the following morning. And I carried all those worries and insecurities with me to school. In fact, I was so absorbed by them I couldn't focus on anything else.

"Amelia?"

Hearing my name shook me from my thoughts. I glanced up to see twenty faces—make that twenty-one, counting Mr. Roybal—staring back at me. I'd been so deep inside my own head, I almost felt startled by my school surroundings. "Wha—what did you say?" I stammered.

"Please pay attention, Ms. Amundsen."

My cheeks burned. "I'm sorry."

Mr. Roybal sighed. "It's all right, Amelia. What I said is that Ms. Horton would like to speak with you."

"Okay," I croaked. "Thanks." My cheeks burned hotter when I noticed a few of the students shooting pitying glances my way. I slid lower in my seat and did my best to not make eye contact with any of them.

I knew what they must be thinking. Winterland was a small town. They'd probably all heard Ryan's nickname for the new girl—Brows—and my ratty appearance was obvious. Here I was the kind of girl who liked carousels and was obsessed with alpacas, when I should've been into shopping and boys and constantly updating a Snapchat account. They had to be thinking I was pathetic.

"Aren't you going to go see her?" Mr. Roybal asked.

"When?"

"Now, of course."

While the class stifled giggles, I realized that Ms. Horton wanting to see me immediately was the type of thing that went without saying in middle school. Everything here moved at a faster and far more structured pace than I was used to. In first grade, it had sometimes taken the better part of an afternoon for the class to get out our snacks, eat baggies filled with carrot slices or Goldfish crackers, and then clean up after ourselves. In seventh grade, snacks were consumed in under five minutes, if they were even allowed.

Apparently, I was out of sync with public school expectations yet again. I'd wrongly assumed that if Ms. Horton wanted to see me, that she'd still want to see me whenever I showed up there. I thought after class, or even after school, would be soon enough. I didn't know it had to be now. Embarrassment weighed down my legs, my arms—my stomach felt especially heavy as I stood from my chair.

"Catherine, will you please make sure Amelia makes it to Ms. Horton's office?" Mr. Roybal said.

At that point, I was too humiliated to speak. Too humiliated to tell Mr. Roybal that I knew where Ms. Horton's office was and that I no longer required an escort. I shot out of the room with Cat not far behind. When she called after me, I hurried on like I didn't hear her. She followed me all the way to Ms. Horton's office anyway. Having her on my tail propelled me forward. It kept me going when what I wanted to do was to curl up in a ball. It wasn't until I marched through the open door that Cat held back.

Ms. Horton lifted her head as soon as I walked in. She cut right to the chase. "Amelia, have you given my letters to your parents yet?"

When I shook my head sheepishly, Ms. Horton selected her red gel pen to write something down in a file—presumably my file. Then she glared at me with her squinty eyes and said, "Well, a decision wouldn't be reached until Principal Stinger is able to interview you and speak with your parents, but in my opinion, your failure to pass along my notes is a clear indicator that you are not ready for middle school. Seventh graders are more responsible than that." She paused as if giving her words time to sink in, then added, "You may go now."

I left Ms. Horton's office feeling even more deflated than when I'd entered. Cat fell into step beside me and whispered, "More responsible than that? Are you kidding me? Does she even know any seventh graders?"

I stopped walking and she did, too. I turned to face her.

"Why don't you like me?" I asked her point blank. "Or do you? I can't tell. You seem to like my brothers. But one minute you're cold to me and the next you're saying something that makes me think maybe you *don't* hate me. All I know is things are weird between us and I don't know why."

Cat stared back at me unflinchingly with her cool gray-blue eyes. "Do you remember the picture you sent me when we were six?"

"What? No." I shook my head. I had no idea what she was talking about.

"It was a drawing of a brick house with rosebushes in front and of a family standing nearby. There were two parents, two boys, and two girls holding hands. You wrote your name above one of the girl's heads, and my name above the other."

As she described the picture, it came back to me. I'd included the drawing in one of the birthday cards my family had sent. It would've been the last card we mailed before we up and sold everything. It seemed like a lifetime ago. Back when we did normal things. Back when I had a room full of toys and crayons, and a head full of my own dreams—things that had been scarce since then.

"I looked at that picture every day for months," Cat said, then glanced away like she could no longer meet my eyes. "It'd always been just me and my grandma, and your drawing made me feel like I was part of a bigger family. It was something I'd always wanted. Whenever I saw other kids drawing pictures of their parents and siblings, I thought I was missing out. And here you were including me with you and your family."

I took a step toward her. I knew what it felt like to want to be included.

"It took me months to get up the courage to write back to you."

"You sent *me a* letter?" I asked, thinking *that* was something I would've remembered.

"Try three. I thought if I asked, you would come visit me and we'd be close—almost like sisters or something. I wanted it so badly. I didn't give up when you didn't respond to the first two letters. But when I invited you a third time, and all I got back was another generic birthday card, I decided it wasn't worth it."

Thoughts swirled inside my head as I tried to keep up. *Cat had written to me? She had invited me to come here?* I could only imagine what had happened to her letters. After we sold our house, it'd been easy to find a post office to send mail but never easy to receive it on the road. How much of our mail had been lost as it had been forwarded around the country? And I never realized how impersonal the birthday cards had been, with only our names scribbled at the bottom.

"*You* never sent me another picture, or letter, or anything. You never made another attempt to be my friend," Cat said, returning her eyes to mine.

Regret drew my gaze to the floor. She was right. Even though I never received her letters, I could've written a note or drawn another picture to slip inside one of her birthday cards. I could've done something these past five years to make us feel less like strangers. But I hadn't.

"And now it's too late," Cat said. With that, she spun on her heel and headed back to class without me. I couldn't think of anything to say to make her stay.

· · ·

The days were starting to add up like wrecked train cars piling on top of one another. I didn't want to go home after school. I wanted to go somewhere where no one would judge me, and where I would feel appreciated instead of like a disappointment. I wanted to go back to the ranch, but I needed to talk to Rachel about a schedule first. So, I rode the bus into town.

I left extra space between myself and the other students getting off the bus. They were caught up in laughter at some joke Ryan was telling. They never glanced back to see me step off behind them. It was the one good thing that had happened to me all day.

I headed straight for Fleece on Earth. Rachel had said to visit later in the week, after she'd had a chance to purchase fence supplies, and we could work out a schedule then. Granted, I wasn't the best at keeping track of days, but even I knew Monday didn't mean "later in the week." But I couldn't wait. I had to know when I could see the alpacas again. I had to have *something* to look forward to.

Instead of Rachel, I found a younger, larger woman with dark skin standing behind the counter. She wore glasses, and her hair was big and curly around her face. There wasn't a hard angle on her anywhere. Her bulging purple T-shirt had an image of three fuzzy alpacas on it. It read PREPARE FOR THE ALPACALYPSE.

I paused just inside the doorway, thinking I might have to come back when Rachel was around, but then the woman smiled and said, "You must be Amelia Jean."

"How . . . how did you know?"

"The scarf," she replied, her voice full of delight.

My fingers shot to my neck. They were instantly rewarded with fluffy softness.

"I hand-knitted that one myself. My mother-in-law said

she'd sold it to you. I also heard about your visit to our ranch last Saturday."

"Your alpacas are amazing. And, oh my goodness, the scarf!" I gushed before getting ahold of myself.

The woman smiled broader.

"Thank you," she said, then reached out to shake my hand. "I'm Julie. Thanks, too, for pitching in. I heard you were very helpful. We've been a little shorthanded these last six months. If nothing else, I know Rachel needs the company." The woman took a deep breath, then cleared her throat as if trying to purge a wave of sadness that had risen from somewhere deep inside her. I remembered what Rachel said about her husband passing away. "And Mom's been extra lonely," Julie added.

"I want to help more!" I blurted out. So much for subtlety. "That's why I'm here. Rachel said we could work out a schedule this week." I left out the "later" part.

"Well," she said before nodding approvingly. "I'm glad Mom found someone with so much enthusiasm to fill the position. Hold on, okay?" She inspected a receipt lying on the counter and then glanced at a calendar hung on the wall behind her. "It looks like Mom placed an order with the hardware store just this morning. The new fence rails won't be in until late Friday afternoon. Can you come by first thing Saturday morning?"

"Yes!" I said. "I'll be there. Thanks!"

It wasn't until after I'd left the shop that the realization of what I'd done set it. My family was planning another long hike for Saturday. They wanted to get an early start, and they were counting on me to come with them. Dad had made it abundantly clear that my job was not to interfere with family adventures.

What am I going to do? My heart sank. If nothing else, the day had proved I was as terrible at managing my day-to-day life as I was at completing dangerous challenges. I so badly wanted to see the alpacas again. And the perfect opportunity was right in front of me. I could work at the ranch on Saturday. There was no good reason I couldn't, except that the rest of my family was determined to climb mountains. It shredded me up inside to know that what I wanted didn't matter.

10

The importation of alpacas into the United States began in 1984.

I was already feeling squeezed by the day's events—my encounter with Ms. Horton, Cat's revelation, my conflicting plans for Saturday . . . Would I get fired if I didn't show up at the ranch? The thought was unbearable. It didn't help that when I climbed into the back of my parents' truck, the cab was overflowing with canvas bags of groceries. There was hardly enough room for me to sit.

"There was a sale on fresh produce," Dad explained. "Do you know how long it's been since I've had a cucumber and tomato salad?"

"Probably more than five years," Mom said wistfully. "Since back when we had our own garden."

Dad cleared his throat. "Anyway, I thought it might be time

to meet some of the neighbors. Thought we could grill outside tonight, invite some people to join us."

I might've thought Dad's comment strange, except I knew he meant our temporary neighbors—other travelers in the RV park. Not the locals or anything. My parents liked to reach out to others living a similar lifestyle. They compared notes on campgrounds, recipes for cramped kitchens, towing capacities, backup generators, and how to get the best Wi-Fi reception on the road.

They turned to one another the way I imagined friends would—drawn together by life circumstances or whatever. They shared conversations and food and stories. And then, save a few exceptions, went their separate ways.

There'd been quite a few times we'd shared meals with families who had kids my age. When I was younger, it'd been easier to pick up a game of tag or hide-and-seek in the RV parks. Nowadays it was just awkward when my parents decided to "meet the neighbors." They always expected me and my brothers to click with the strangers. Neil and David were better at it than I was. They'd go on and on about how they someday wanted to free solo El Capitan, or at least reach the top of Denali. They'd talk to anyone who'd listen. I never knew what to say.

I groaned inwardly, so my parents wouldn't hear me from the front seat. Dealing with strangers would only add to the pressure I was under. And it didn't stop there. "Should we invite Catherine and her grandmother, too?" Dad asked. The hope in his voice drove me down further. "Your mother and I would still like to meet them."

Cat's words echoed in my head: *It's too late.*

"Uh," I said. "I don't think that's a good idea." I scrambled to come up with an explanation. "She wasn't feeling well at school today."

"Oh, okay," Dad said disappointedly. "Too bad."

"Yeah, too bad," I said, then diverted my gaze so Dad couldn't catch my eyes in the rearview mirror.

I lucked out. The RV park was almost empty. My parents were only able to rope in a young couple without any children to share dinner with my family. They hardly noticed when I excused myself from the circle of lawn chairs and retreated inside the Gnarly Banana.

The rest of my family didn't come in until it was nearly dark. When they did, they were practically buzzing with excitement. "What's going on?" I asked.

"The Zhangs run a popular travel blog. After we told them about the Amundsen Adventure Jar, they invited us to be guest bloggers and to write about our experiences. They said they've been looking for a family to provide a different perspective on RV living, and they think we're a perfect match! Isn't that exciting?" Dad was nearly breathless, but he kept talking. "It pays some. Not much . . . I'll have to crunch some numbers, but maybe we can get back on the road even sooner than I was anticipating."

Neil let out a whoop. Mom squeezed Dad's hand. David's face lit up, too, but then his eyes drifted toward the window. He must've been thinking about Annie, our nameless dog, because his smile faltered a bit.

"I mean, we still need to tackle the next challenge, but I'll start looking into other mountain ranges. We have plenty of options for skiing a black diamond. If the blogging thing works out, there's no reason for us to stay in Colorado much longer than a few more weeks."

A few more weeks? My stomach rose, then dipped, like the animals on the carousel. What about my job at the alpaca ranch? There was no way Rachel and I could complete the fence repair in a few weeks. Especially if I had to cancel on her for the hike on Saturday . . . unless Dad made an exception for me again so I wouldn't have to.

I opened my mouth to speak but lost my nerve. I told myself I didn't want to put a damper on their good mood. It could wait until tomorrow. As for Ms. Horton, why put anyone through the misery of meeting with Principal Stinger if we were hitting the road again anyway?

But the following evening, my family was gathered around the laptop looking at a ski resort in Wyoming. The night after, they had trail maps out and were debating the best routes to prepare for climbing the fourteener, and when and which fourteener to climb.

I nearly panicked when Neil suggested we relocate to somewhere near Aspen, Colorado, and the Elk Mountains so we could scramble across something called the "Knife Edge on Capitol Peak." But then Mom jumped in and reminded him that we were trying to be more "economical" in our travels and not spend as much on gas.

"Better for the environment that way, too," David piped in, and I wondered if he was really thinking about gas, or if he wasn't ready to leave Annie behind.

The days passed quickly, and I hadn't said a thing about me working on the ranch instead of hiking on Saturday. On Friday night I finally cornered Dad in the trailer while everyone else was outside. "Dad," I said, "about the hike—"

"Don't worry about it, Amelia Jean. Neil and David wanted to skip ahead and climb a fourteener tomorrow. We've been here long enough that our bodies should've adjusted to living at a higher altitude by now. I talked them out of it, though. The hike we're doing has a steep elevation climb, but it's shorter and we'll only reach about twelve thousand feet."

"But—"

"It's okay," Dad said. "None of us really mind doing another, easier hike this Saturday. We want you to feel comfortable. And it's important that you have a chance to condition yourself, since you missed last week's hike."

I forced the corners of my lips to rise and nodded my head. "Thanks." I hated myself for it, but I just couldn't bring myself to confess that I'd committed to working at the ranch and a hike on the same day.

Then, early Saturday morning, when Dad already had my hydration pack pulled out of our extra storage container at the front of the trailer, and my brothers were packing up sandwiches Mom made at the deli to bring with us, and Mom was telling me to put on my hiking boots, well . . . by then it felt too late, and I sort of understood Cat's point. Sometimes life and time piled up until it felt like an opportunity was no longer available.

The words sat on the tip of my tongue anyway; they just sat there. They remained—just waiting for me to find the courage to ask. As we drove by Rachel's ranch and I saw Lulu and Benny, Chai Latte, and the others with their heads lifting to watch us pass, I pressed my fingers to the glass. I was so worried Rachel would fire me for missing work today, and I'd never get to see the alpacas again. I wanted to scream, "Let me out!" But I couldn't.

My family was soaring through life, with sails perpetually set for adventure. And what it boiled down to was I couldn't stand to be an anchor. Not again. My best hope was that we'd finish the hike early and that there'd be enough time for me to work at the ranch when we got back.

. . .

We parked in a dirt lot near the trailhead. It wasn't until we hopped out of the truck that I could get a good look at where we were headed. The mountain peak loomed impossibly high above us. My brothers bumped fists. When I glanced up, it filled my stomach with dread.

Dad noticed me grimacing and clapped me on the back. "One step at a time," he said. We did a final check to be sure we had everything—hydration packs, rain gear, extra layers of clothing, first aid packs, and lunch—and then we were off.

My brothers trucked ahead while my parents hung back with me. They didn't say I was slowing them down, but I could tell I was. They carried on a conversation. I was too winded, or maybe just too disappointed, to speak.

Mom inhaled deeply. "Ah, I love breathing this crisp mountain air."

"Yep. Feels good to get the blood pumping," Dad said.

"I'm looking forward to writing again," Mom said. "And

something inspirational . . . Not that my closing arguments weren't persuasive . . ." Mom didn't have the same distinguished-looking eyebrows as the rest of us. However, she could employ her thinner, lighter brows to do amazing things. She arched one in a cunning curve as she spoke. "But they weren't the sort of thing most people would consider enjoyable reading. Writing for the Zhangs' blog will be different. Fun, I think."

"I know exactly what you mean. It'll feel good to be contributing to something," Dad piped in. "You know, feeling productive, and like we're a part of something bigger. I've missed that."

My stomach churned. Working at the alpaca ranch felt good. It made me feel like I was part of something bigger. But listening to my parents—it would take getting back on the road for them to feel that sort of satisfaction. I hated that my happiness and their happiness always seemed to be at odds. Lost in thought, I stumbled on a small rock, and Mom turned to check on me.

"Are you feeling all right, honey?" Mom asked. "You're looking a little pale."

"My stomach hurts. Not too bad, though," I said. "Maybe it's the altitude."

Concern trickled onto Mom's face. She scrunched up her forehead. "Okay. Let me know if it gets worse. Altitude sickness is nothing to mess around with."

By then, we'd been hiking for several hours. There were fewer and fewer trees as we gained elevation on the mountain. Without the forest to block the wind, we kept getting blasted by gusts of frigid air. Plus, there were trip hazards galore as the dirt trail shifted to jagged steps made from large rocks and boulders. I kept my eyes glued to my feet and trudged along.

"Slow and steady," Dad said. "It's as much a mental feat as a physical one. Just think how good you'll feel when you reach the top."

Will I? Feel good, that is . . . I knew my parents and brothers would feel a rush of something when they summited. But it was hard to get excited about something that wasn't on my own bucket list, especially when I was feeling guilty for ditching Rachel. Was she wondering where I was? Had she dropped by our trailer looking for me? Maybe her daughter-in-law forget to mention that I'd agreed to work today. But I doubted that. Rachel had been so kind to me. I'd stood her up in return.

My stomach revolted on me again. I sipped on the hose from my hydration pack and tried to relax. Then I rounded a bend and was hit with a view that made my head spin. The side of the mountain fell away. I could see for miles and miles. It was breathtaking and terrifying all at once. It was at least a level four on my fear rating scale.

The exposure to heights didn't seem to bother my parents

in the slightest. And Neil and David must've whizzed right by since they were nowhere to be seen. Mom and Dad paused a moment to take in the sights, then started walking and chatting again, like it was no big deal that a stumble could send one of us (I was the most likely candidate!) plummeting over the edge. I knew they'd just be bemused if I said anything—like the thought hadn't crossed their minds—so I hugged the non-steep side of the trail and crept on.

The hike wasn't all misery. The views were amazing, and I especially liked the little creatures that kept popping up once we were past the tree line. Mom said they were called "pikas." They reminded me of little bunnies, only with rounded mouse ears. They made sharp chirping noises before scurrying back into their holes.

We also came across three white mountain goats. They were somehow both muscular and fluffy. Their pointed horns and buff bodies were more than a little intimidating. Luckily, they showed way more interest in grazing and hanging out on the rocky cliffside than in me and my parents.

I thought I was making okay progress, all things considered, until Dad stopped in his tracks, scanned the sky, and said, "Amelia Jean, you're gonna have to pick up the pace. I don't like all these clouds rolling in."

I turned my eyes upward. A cotton ball haze was beginning

to sponge out the blue skies, but the billowing clouds looked pillow soft and far less threatening than the jagged rocks we'd have to scramble over to reach the mountaintop.

Regardless, I quickened my step for a few meters before my body resisted moving forward and climbing up. I fell back into a slump and dragged my feet up the trail.

When Mom glanced over her shoulder and noticed the growing distance between me and them, she nudged my father. Dad swiveled between measuring the distance to the peak and worriedly gazing back at me. "Let's go, Amelia Jean!" he prodded.

Neil and David were waiting for us at the top by a crystal clear mountain lake. It appeared out of place to me, so high on the mountain, surrounded by craggy walls of rock.

"What took you guys so long?" Neil asked. Then his eyes grazed mine and he quickly changed the subject. "We should eat," he said. "Quickly. Before the weather changes."

My brothers had packed in our lunches. I found a place between two boulders, where I was sheltered from the wind. I was starving. As such, I nearly inhaled my ham and provolone on ciabatta bread, washed it down with sips from my hydration pack, then unwrapped a chocolate chip cookie from cellophane.

David was watching me. "Yeah, hiking makes me hungry, too," he said kindly. Being the middle child, David bridged more than the age difference between Neil and me. David loved heart-pulsing action and excitement every bit as much as Neil. But he was quieter, less intense. No doubt, he gravitated more toward Neil most of the time. But every now and then, he'd say or do something that made me feel included. I grinned back at him and polished off the chocolate chip cookie.

My parents and Neil were seeking shelter on the opposite side of one of the boulders. The wind drowned out their voices. I knew it would drown out mine and David's, too. My stomach felt better, and I'd shed some of the guilt and worry I'd been carrying around with me all morning. There was nothing I could do now about standing Rachel up.

"Do you like it here?" I asked. When you shared a trailer the size of a large bedroom with four other people, there weren't many opportunities to speak to any of them alone. I didn't know what my family members really thought of Winterland. But if anyone else was having doubts about leaving, it would be David. I'd seen the sad look he got in his eyes whenever Annie wagged her tail and stared up at him like he was the most wonderful person on the face of the earth.

"Yeah," David said. "It's prettier here than the place we hiked to last week."

"That's not what I meant," I said. "Do you like it here, in Winterland?"

Sometimes I forgot that David wasn't eons older than me. It'd always been the two of them, David and Neil, the boys in the family, and I'd felt separate because I was a girl and because I was the youngest. But David was fourteen. He was barely out of middle school.

He nodded, looking uncharacteristically vulnerable. "I do. I like . . . Don't laugh, okay?" The shy smile on his face made him look even younger somehow.

"I won't."

"I like high school. I joined a rock-climbing club, and there's all these other after-school activities and electives. And I like being around other ninth graders. Neil and I are tight, but he's always a step ahead of me. At school, the other kids are impressed with all the places I've been and things I've done. It's nice. I'm sure it's the same for you."

We never talked like this and I didn't want him to stop, so I didn't interrupt and tell him that, no, it was nothing like that for me.

"Then there's . . . Annie," he said.

I offered him a sympathetic smile. "I know."

His face clouded. "I don't want to leave her." His voice cracked and he looked kinda embarrassed about me seeing him so upset.

"I know," I said again. "I don't want to leave her, either."

"She's always so happy to see us. We earned her trust and we're just going to leave her behind? It doesn't seem right." David sniffled before shifting and straightening his position on the hard, uneven ground. Then it was like someone flipped a switch and he was back to being my invincible brother. "It's worth it, though," he said in the more soldier-like voice I was used to hearing from him. "How many people get to see the country the way we do? There are going to be sacrifices, right? But it's worth it," he said a second time, and I wondered if he was trying to convince me or himself.

Maybe for him, it didn't matter. He'd miss Annie, but David's open and friendly manner won him friends wherever he went. And Neil's boldness commanded respect. *It was so simple for them to break the ice with Cat*, I thought with a touch of jealousy. Was it really too late for me, though? The entire way up, I thought I'd never make it to the top of this mountain, yet here I was. What if there was a way for Cat and me to still be friends? I decided to ask my brother for pointers.

"David—" I started, then Dad popped his head around the boulder.

"Time to roll!" he said.

A large drop of rain splattered on the rock beside me, turning it slick and dark. Then another and another. Lightning severed the sky. Thunder cracked the air. I jumped to my feet, slithered into my rain gear, and quickly gathered my belongings.

"Come on, kids," Mom said. She sounded nervous, and Mom never sounded nervous unless we were in real danger. She trusted herself. She trusted the equipment we used on our adventures. But the one thing Mom said she never trusted was nature. Nature was unpredictable. Nature could be deadly. "We need to move. NOW!"

Next thing I knew, we were racing down the side of the mountain. Another bolt of lightning splintered the clouds, followed seconds later by a crackling boom. A jolt of fear coursed through me, and I ran faster. I ran like I was running for my life—because maybe I was.

11

Alpacas are sheared once a year, in the spring.
Each shearing produces approximately five to ten
pounds of fiber.

The best thing to do in a lightning storm is to get indoors, but anything remotely resembling "indoors" was miles away. Dad held back and ushered me in front of him on the narrow trail. "We have to get down quickly, find some cover. But don't get careless. Watch your feet."

Caution, fear, and panic swirled inside me, nearly bringing up my lunch. The rain-soaked rocks were slippery, and the freezing droplets blurred my vision. I shivered while trying to hurry and while trying to keep my wits about me, and while trying to keep track of my footing.

"That's it, Amelia Jean." Dad raised his voice to be heard above the storm. "Keep moving." More deft and agile than me, Mom and my brothers were speeding ahead.

I hurried around a bend and hit a patch of wet, loose stone and gravel. My feet lost connection with the ground. My arms shot out in a desperate attempt to grab hold of something, but it was no use. The rain had washed the trail right out from under me.

The world went slanted. I thought, *This is going to hurt.* The worst of it was that the downpour had so completely veiled my view that I had no idea where I was going to land. Or even how far I would fall.

Then Dad swooped in from nowhere, looped his arms around my midsection, and pulled me close. "Gotcha," he said, unable to mask the quaver in his voice. As he lowered me to a safer, more stable part of the trail that hadn't been swept away by the storm, I caught a glimpse of where I'd been headed—straight down a steep, rocky drop-off.

"Are you okay?" he asked, positioning himself directly in front of me, blocking my view of the tumble I'd almost taken.

I nodded inside the hood of my raincoat. I couldn't speak.

"Good. Disaster avoided, right?" he said, peeking out from his own hood and looking straight into my eyes. I tried to summon the courage I knew he wanted to find there, but I couldn't. I just couldn't.

His jaw tightened. He hadn't shaved that morning and the stubble on his chin was dark with flecks of gray.

The sky split with lightning again and I jerked in fright.

Dad rested his hand on my shoulder. "We're not safe here, not like this." He paused, thinking. "And we're not safe rushing down like before. So . . . new plan. You and I aren't going to beat the weather off the mountain. Instead, we'll wait it out. But we need to find a lower spot, somewhere we can crouch down. All right?"

I followed him, going slightly off trail, away from any trees, and shrank down like he showed me in a depressed section of ground—with all my weight resting on the balls of my feet. The rain slid off my jacket. I hugged my knees to my chest. Every time the thunder clapped, I shook harder. But eventually, the deluge lightened. The booms sounded farther in the distance. At last, the storm cleared.

• • •

On the ride home, my brothers seemed energized by the experience. "That was definitely Type Two Fun!" Neil said. According to him, there were three types of fun. Type One, which was pure fun—enjoyable while it was happening. Type Two, which wasn't fun in the moment but was fun to relive in the memories. And Type Three, which was no fun at all.

I had to disagree. It had been a strong Type Three for me.

"We definitely have to get an earlier start when we hike the fourteener," Dad said. I caught a glimpse of myself in Dad's rearview mirror. All the blood had drained from my face. My clothes hadn't dried yet, my body still ached, and I was far from recovered from the fright of this hike, yet my family was already planning the next. If Dad hadn't rescued me when I slipped, I might not have survived. How would I ever survive climbing a fourteener?

"That storm was not in the forecast. It blew in so quickly," Dad continued.

"That's why it's best to hike in the morning," Mom said. "Afternoon weather is so unpredictable at this altitude."

Dad nodded solemnly. "You're absolutely right. I just underestimated how long it would take for us to reach the top."

Mom and Dad shared a look, and I knew what they were thinking. I was the reason it had taken so long for us to reach the top. So I was the reason we'd been caught in the storm. If not for me, the rest of them would've been off the mountain when the first raindrop hit. Not only that, the time Dad and I spent cowering beside the trail cost us hours. There wouldn't be enough daylight left when we made it back for me to visit the ranch.

It'd been a lousy day, and what ate at me the most was knowing how else I could've spent it. I could've been at the ranch, happily helping Rachel and feeling more than comfortable surrounded by alpacas. Instead, I was wet and tired and gnawed by fear. Not only that, my family would never have been caught in the storm if I hadn't been there. We were all worse off because I hadn't had the courage to speak up. But even if I had known it would turn out this way, I don't think I would've been able to do things differently. Because that's who I was—a coward.

. . .

After Mom left for the deli the next day, Dad got called in for an extra shift at the market. One of the cashiers was out with the summer flu. Being the one with the least seniority, Dad was expected to fill in. He was in a sour mood after hanging up with his boss. "I wanted to fit in a second day of conditioning. I don't know if we're ready to tackle a fourteener next weekend," he grumbled. And by "we" I knew he meant me. "Don't want anyone running out of stamina on the mountain."

My brothers would never run out of stamina, but Neil piped in, "The high school's rock-climbing club is meeting in the canyon today for some bouldering. If we're not hiking again, at least David and I can fit in some climbing."

Dad nodded approvingly. "I'll drop you off on my way in."

I could tell the second it dawned on him that if my brothers were at a club activity, I'd be left alone, because he furrowed his brow. We'd never run into these types of scheduling dilemmas before, and he didn't seem too pleased. "What about you, Amelia Jean?"

I'd been moping around since the day before. But in that moment, inspiration struck, and I bolted upright in my seat. "I can work at the ranch," I said. I hadn't spoken with Rachel about it, but maybe I could make up for missing work the day before.

Dad mulled it over. I knew it wasn't what he wanted for me, but in his mind any physical activity was better than me lying around the trailer all day. To nudge him in the right direction, I added, "And maybe I can take An— I mean, the dog, and we can walk to the ranch. So I can get some extra exercise."

When the creases on his forehead grew deeper, I worried that mentioning the dog had been a mistake. Thankfully, his brow soon loosened, and he said, "I guess." He must've realized I'd be safer with a large dog by my side to ward off any mountain lions or coyotes in the area. "Just don't wander off into the forest. And try to jog a little on your way there and back. Stretch your lungs."

I grinned and said, "Sounds good." It sounded great, actually.

Dad hesitated for a split second like he might change his mind. I held my breath, willing him not to. Finally, he shook his head sadly and said, "You're growing up too fast." Then he squeezed me in a quick hug before he and my brothers exited the Gnarly Banana. I followed them out the door, down the steps, and then waved them off.

Annie chased after the truck for a few hundred feet before circling back to where I was standing. I briefly wondered if one of these times, she wouldn't come back. I knew that's what Dad was hoping for. But for now, apparently, she had adopted our family.

I scratched behind her ears. "Want to go see some alpacas, girl? Huh? Do you?" Annie panted and wagged her tail excitedly. "You do, don't you?"

Dad's bad luck (being called in for an extra shift) was my good fortune. I couldn't believe that in the span of a few minutes, I'd gone from having to spend the day adventuring with Dad and my brothers to being completely free. I wanted to kiss his boss and the employee who'd called in sick.

A few minutes after the family truck disappeared down the road, I had Annie's makeshift leash and collar around her neck, and my ratty tennis shoes on my feet. Normally, I hated to jog, but time was limited. Mom was working a half shift and would be back in four hours. She'd be worried if I wasn't waiting for her at the trailer.

I sped off down the gravel road and out to the paved street. Annie kept pace with me, and occasionally glanced my way. *This is fun, right?* her eyes seemed to say. *We should do this more often.*

It wasn't fun. I liked running only slightly more than I liked rappelling off cliffs, but I jogged all the way to Rachel's ranch. And I knew if Dad could see me, he would be proud. I was stretching my lungs, just like he'd suggested.

With Annie by my side, the alpacas kept their distance from the fence. It wasn't until I reached the end of Rachel's long dirt drive, looped Annie's rope leash around a porch post, found a water bowl to leave beside her, and put a decent gap between myself and the dog that they wanted anything to do with me.

I carefully opened and slid through the gate the way Rachel had shown me. Benny was the first alpaca to approach. He eyed me curiously, with great big eyes and a smile. I knew it wasn't the same as a human smile. All alpacas had stubby snouts and lips that curled upward. They all had permanent smiles. But still. It warmed my heart. Benny's smile made me feel appreciated, even if it was the same look he gave everyone.

"Hey, buddy," I said, and stroked the soft, soft fur on the back of his neck. At the same time, I felt a tug. I turned my head to find Carl sniffing, er, eating? my ponytail. I gently pulled my hair away and gathered it to one side. "Sorry, no treats today. Not yet, at least."

I scanned the fields for Rachel but saw only alpacas. There was a vehicle and trailer I hadn't seen the time before parked next to the barn. My stomach dropped. Maybe Rachel found someone else to fill the position after I'd stood her up. I wouldn't blame her, but it would crush me to see another person doing the job I so badly wanted.

Nonetheless, I made my way toward the barn. At very least, I owed Rachel an explanation. As I rounded the corner, a glob of something slimy hit my cheek. I swiped with my hand and smeared the goo all over my fingers. Trying to make sense of what had happened, I glanced from the sticky substance gelling together chunks of grass to the two alpacas and the two human faces peering back at me.

"Amelia!" Rachel said. "I'm so sorry."

"Is this . . . spit?" I asked.

Rachel stifled a chuckle and nodded. "I'm afraid it is. But Sky wasn't aiming for you."

The stranger in the barn cleared his throat. "I guess that's good news, then," he said quietly. "I'll just load up my herdsire and we'll be on our way."

"Thank you," Rachel said, and shook his hand. Instead of a collar and rope leash like we used on Annie, a halter was wrapped around the alpaca's snout and head, and the leash clipped beneath his chin.

While the man gently led the larger alpaca out of the barn, Rachel handed me a handkerchief to wipe myself clean. I nearly burst waiting for the stranger to leave. "If Sky wasn't aiming her spit at me, who was she aiming at?"

Rachel's eyes were gleaming as she focused her gaze on my now clean face. Something was making her happy, and I couldn't understand what considering I'd just been slimed. Not to mention she had every right to be angry with me. "That was a spit-off," she said.

"Um, yeah." I peered around Rachel to the alpaca standing in the pen behind her. I hadn't been introduced to Sky the previous week. She was one of the fluffiest alpacas I'd seen. Her fleece was a silver gray. She shied away from my stare. Unlike the friendlier alpacas I'd met, Sky wanted nothing to do with me. It was hard not to take the spit assault, er, spit-off personally.

"Why doesn't she like me?" I asked.

"Sky? No, she is more hesitant than Lulu and Benny and some of the others I've had for a while. Don't worry, though; she'll warm up once she gets to know you."

A seed of hope sprouted inside me. Did that mean Rachel wasn't angry, that she still wanted me around? Then another thought arrived like a bitter aftertaste: Would I be around long enough for Sky to warm up to me? Who knew with Dad? He wasn't happy with his job and now that he had an alternative with the Zhangs' blog, he was antsy to get on the road again.

Sky hummed, drawing me out of my thoughts. But it wasn't

the cheerful noise I'd heard from Samson as he bounded around his mother. "Is she going to spit me off again?"

"Oh, I highly doubt it. And, like I said, she wasn't spitting *you* off. You just happened to be standing the same vicinity as her actual target." Rachel was still grinning broadly. Confusion must've shown on my face, because she went on, "Remember last week when I told you we'd know soon if we had another cria like Samson on the way? Well, the spit-off just confirmed it. Sky and Mr. Kelly's herdsire haven't seen each other since we coupled them a month ago. Sky wasn't spitting at you. She was spitting at the stud."

I shook my head. None of this was making any sense.

"She was telling him to back off," Rachel added. "Sky was telling him that she's pregnant."

"Oh," I said. And then I let out a louder, more excited "OH!" Another baby alpaca? No wonder Rachel looked so happy. "How long? Until the cria is born, I mean."

"Not for close to a year, I'm afraid. The gestation period for alpacas is eleven to twelve months."

My heart sank. Even if Sky did warm up to me, there was no way I'd be around long enough to meet her baby. Rachel must've seen the disappointment in my eyes, because she said, "Come on. Let's give Sky some peace and quiet and go check on Samson."

Samson was every bit as adorable as I remembered. He had

hay in his bangs, a grin on his face, and far more energy than his mother. He ran circles around the pen while his mother ate hay from the feeder.

"You've fed them already," I noted.

"Yes, Julie gave me a hand with it earlier."

"Oh," I said quietly. "I'm glad. Maybe next time I'll be able to come sooner so I don't miss out." I snuck a sidelong glance at her.

Her attention was on the alpacas still, so I couldn't quite read her expression. "We missed you yesterday," she said, but not unkindly. "The posts and hardware for the fence arrived on Friday . . ." She trailed off as if wanting me to fill in the blanks about my absence.

A wave of guilt washed over me. "I'm so sorry I wasn't here," I said. I owed her an explanation. But with so many emotions swirling within me, I didn't know how to pull them apart and form the right words. I was disappointed in myself for not telling my family how important it was for me to work at the ranch. At the same time, I hadn't wanted to let them down. So I'd gone on the hike, all the while wanting to be here but being afraid to say so. Conflicts like this were new to me, and so were things like commitments to people outside my family.

"I'm not good with schedules," I blurted out. A sickening feeling hit when the two letters from Ms. Horton, and the still unscheduled interview, sprang to mind. "Seriously, I'm terrible at them. But I *really* want this job, and I promise I will come whenever I can. Please don't fire me," I begged.

Rachel pursed her lips together while I wiped beads of sweat from my forehead and held my breath. After what felt like forever, she cracked a smile. "Fortunately, we're pretty laid back around here. A flexible schedule should work just fine."

A rush of air escaped my lungs. "Thank you! Thank you SO much."

"I should warn you, however; there's something we need to take care of before starting on the fence today, and you might find the work somewhat . . ." She paused as if searching for the right word. She finally settled on, "Unpleasant."

I gulped. "That's okay," I said. After standing her up the day before, I felt like unpleasant work might be preferable to carrying around buckets of guilt. And, either way, whatever it was, I'd still be here on the ranch. Near the alpacas.

She glanced down at my ratty tennis shoes and then at her own galoshes. "What size of shoe do you wear, Amelia Jean?"

"Seven and a half," I said. I had big feet for a girl my age. It went along with the height.

"Wonderful! You can borrow Julie's boots, so your shoes won't get messy."

I refrained from pointing out that my shoes weren't worth saving. "All right," I said. I swapped out my sneakers for Julie's galoshes in the barn. Then Rachel handed me a shovel while she retrieved a wheelbarrow. "Time to collect some manure," she said.

I winced, but it wasn't a total surprise. I'd suspected the "unpleasant" work needing to be completed today would be something along those lines.

Turns out, alpacas are pretty tidy animals. They used what Rachel called "a communal dung pile" to relieve themselves. The pile was in one corner of the field, away from where the herd of alpacas had gathered.

"I've heard you can potty train them to use litter boxes," Rachel said. "Although I've never been inclined to try."

"Hmm," I said, staring at the pile and wondering how difficult it would be to train them to go in a box. Might be worth it. At least their waste didn't stink *that* bad. And the pile wasn't *that* big. And it didn't take *that* long to remove. The worst part was how squishy it was when I dug the shovel in.

As we rolled it back to the barn and went about transferring the waste into buckets, Rachel said, "Alpaca manure makes for awesome garden fertilizer. It's rich in nutrients and it enhances the soil composition. We have more orders for it than we can usually fill, and it provides a decent chunk of income for the ranch. Plus, it's not nearly as smelly as what comes out the back end of a cow or horse."

I giggled. "Shoveling horse manure—now that would be an unpleasant job," I said.

"There's a reason I stick to alpacas," Rachel fired back.

After we finished filling the buckets, we examined where the fence was weak and eroding. Wood was rotted, posts were split, and nails were rusted. In some places a hard shove would've collapsed an entire section. With a stroke of red paint, Rachel marked all the rails requiring replacement (thirty-three in all). Then she pointed out the new rails where they were stacked behind Samson and Hazel's pen.

Next, we were off to the barn to retrieve tools—hammers, saws, eye protection, and items I'd never seen before. Rachel demonstrated how to pry the first rotten rail from the fence and the rusty nails free—with a great deal of force, a crowbar, and a pair of pliers. Once the old rail was removed, she measured for a new one, sawed it at the appropriate mark, then secured it between the existing posts. Each step took a significant amount of time and energy.

"There," Rachel said. "One down."

One down? All that effort for one single rail and we had thirty-two to go? My head was swimming. The task seemed more difficult and vast than I'd imagined. I hadn't expected anything on the ranch to feel as intimidating as facing a roiling ocean wave or staring over the lip of a canyon. But this did.

"While I remove the next rail, you measure and saw its replacement," Rachel instructed.

"*What*?" I croaked. "Me?" Before today, I couldn't remember the last time I'd touched a saw or a hammer. What if I sawed off a finger or smashed my thumb? "No. I can't."

"Why can't you? Everything you need is right in front of you," she said. "And you have youthful exuberance on your side. Give it a shot. See what happens." Rachel winked at me, then set about removing the next rail.

I reminded myself how badly I wanted this job. Plus, I'd agreed to helping with the fence repair before Rachel ordered the supplies. I couldn't back out now, so I took a deep breath and dove in. I struggled. I hefted. I measured. I sawed. I was clumsy at it—the board slipped this way and that—and my cut turned out ragged and ugly. My arm ached by the time the rail split apart. But, eventually, I lugged my handiwork over to Rachel. As I helped her lift the rail into place, a wave of gratification washed over me. I did it! I felt good. I felt proud. That was, until the rail came up an airy inch short.

The failure hit me harder than it should've. Lately I'd been messing up all over the place. I was a flop at school. My cousin resented me. My dad had needed to rescue me on the past two family adventures. But not here. Not at the ranch. The ranch was supposed to be my sanctuary—the one place I didn't screw things up.

"Argh, no!" I shouted at the blue sky between the rail and the post it was supposed to reach. I kicked a rock and pain shot through my big toe, up my leg. Dad was right, I had no business working here. Not because it was hard, or because I'd rather spend my time doing other things, but because I was worthless at it.

I was as worthless at working on the ranch as I was at rappelling and hiking up mountains, and at making friends. My heavy heart collapsed me into a puddle of disappointment. "I can't do it," I said. Feeding the alpacas and even shoveling manure was easy. But this—fence repair—took abilities I didn't possess. I should've known better. I wasn't skilled at anything. "You should probably find someone else," I grumbled.

Rachel lowered herself to the ground beside me. "Don't tell me I misjudged you."

I raised my eyes to meet hers. "What do you mean?" I asked hesitantly. I was afraid I'd let her down like everyone else.

"I mean, I didn't take you for the type of person who gives up so easily."

"Oh . . . but you hardly know me," I said. I wasn't even sure myself. Did I give up easily?

"That's not true. I do know you. You're resilient, you're kind, you're loyal, and you're strong."

"Me?" I eyed her with more than a little disbelief.

"You are," she said assuredly. "You're resilient. The first time I met you, you were lost, but you found your way home, didn't you? You're kind. The alpacas wouldn't respond to you the way they do if you weren't. You're loyal. For whatever reason, you missed work yesterday, but you're here now. You're strong. It hurt when that boy made fun of you, but you brushed yourself off and you took this job. And I'm glad you did. I think you're the exact right person for it."

I wanted to think those things were true, but I still wasn't convinced. "Maybe, but I'm not . . . skilled. I don't know how to use tools or equipment, or—" I cut myself off before saying "how to make friends."

"All the skill in the world won't get you anywhere unless you have grit, Amelia Jean. In most cases, grit is the determining factor. And I think you have plenty of it. So, what do you say? Want to give it another go?"

My chest heaved as I drew in air and blew it out. I didn't answer Rachel, but I stood and retrieved another rail. I measured the distance, then I measured again. "'Short cuts make long delays.'" I whispered Tolkien's words to myself. *Literally*, I thought. Then, despite myself, I smiled softly.

This time the sawing was every bit as hard, but I held the wood firmly, and I didn't stop. My cut turned out smoother. And when I helped Rachel lift the rail into place, it fit like a glove.

I smiled smugly and so did Rachel. "Well done," she said. "I think that's enough for today. The rest can wait. Why don't we go spend some time with the alpacas instead? We deserve it. Plus, I think Lulu is feeling starved for attention."

Sure enough, Lulu came right up to us as soon as we entered the pen. Then she did something Rachel called "cushing." She folded her legs beneath her. She was lying down, sort of, with her head and long neck held in an upright position. She batted her eyelashes.

Rachel laughed. "That means she wants to be petted. Not all alpacas like to be touched, but Lulu is definitely an exception." We crouched down beside her. I stroked Lulu's neck and ran my fingers down the soft fur on her back. Every time I stopped, Lulu turned her head toward me and batted those long eyelashes until I started again.

A dreamy expression bloomed on Rachel's face. "My husband and I used to spend hours together out here with the alpacas. He was Lulu's favorite. I think she might miss him almost as much as I do."

"I'm sorry," I said, not sure what else I could say.

Rachel's chest heaved and then she sighed and said, "I'm

not. The hurt and the hole left inside me is deeper than anything I've felt in my life. But I'm so very glad it happened. I'm so very thankful for the time my husband and I shared and the memories we made. No matter how long or how short, it's the connections we make with others that matter most. Connections make life worth living."

Adventures make life worth living," Dad said as he dreamily flipped through a *National Geographic* magazine he'd brought home with him from the market.

I wondered who was right—Dad or Rachel? Was it adventure or connection that kept people going? Couldn't it be both?

"And I'll tell you what," Dad added. "Nothing sucks the life out of you like a bad day at work."

"Hear! Hear!" Mom chimed in. She was lying down on her and Dad's bed with a cool washcloth draped across her forehead.

I kept my mouth shut.

It was Neil's night to cook. The cramped kitchen was only large enough for one body, so we all took turns. The rest of us were scattered around the front of the trailer while my oldest brother had a pot of water boiling on the tiny stove and a pan of tomato and meat sauce warming on a hot plate on the counter. The sauce came from a jar, but Neil was adding fresh basil and minced garlic to spice it up. Of all of us, he liked cooking the most. But the trailer kitchen didn't allow much room for culinary experimentation.

"You know, some of the newer travel trailers have pop-outs and enough space for kitchen islands," Neil said.

Dad groaned. "Not tonight, Neil."

Mom, no doubt trying to turn the tide of negativity flowing through the Gnarly Banana, sat up and said, "And how was bouldering today, boys?"

"Sweet," David answered.

"Indeed." Neil whooped. "Sunday Wild Exertion, Enjoyed Thoroughly."

Then the conversation descended into a jumble of words that didn't hold my interest. Some of them floated into my consciousness: crags, *grip holds*, *technique*, *finger tape*. But mostly, my mind wandered back to Rachel's alpaca ranch and my success with the fence. We had a long way to go, but I was excited to see how it progressed.

I was in my own separate world until a lull in the conservation, followed by Dad asking "What about you, Amelia Jean? How was your day?" shook me from my thoughts.

"Um, it was okay," I said. Sure, it'd been hard, and I felt exhausted, but also satisfied and accomplished. I learned I was capable of more than I thought I was. But I didn't think that's what Dad wanted to hear—not when that revelation had come from working at the ranch and not from one of our family adventures. So, I focused on something I knew would please him. "I ran all the way to the ranch and back."

"Attagirl," he said, nodding approvingly.

"I think I'll start jogging after school *every* day," I added, knowing exactly where those jogs would lead me.

Dad perked up. "Really, Amelia Jean? I didn't think you cared much for it."

"Well, the scenery is so pretty here. And I like being outdoors."

Dad looked at me with a mixture of surprise and delight, like maybe I really was his daughter after all. Like all these years there'd been a little nagging doubt in the back of his head that he hadn't passed on any strong Amundsen genes to me. But now? "That's great. Really great," he said. "It'll help you get ready for hiking the fourteener."

"That's what I was thinking," I said cheerfully, while the words *What is wrong with me?* popped into my head. That wasn't at all what I was thinking.

I went on pandering to Dad anyway. "I'll get off at the RV

park bus stop every day instead of staying on the bus all the way into town and catching a ride home with you and Mom. I should be back from my jog around the same time you get home." While I was talking, I was calculating how much time I'd be able to work at the ranch each afternoon—about an hour. Long enough to replace a rail or two each day. I returned Dad's smile.

"Good plan, Amelia Jean," Dad said. "You do that each day this week, and you'll be surprised by how much energy and stamina you'll have for the hike on Saturday. And it's nice to see you managing your time and commitments so well."

Dad's praise jogged my memory—I still hadn't given the letters from Ms. Horton to my parents. They didn't know we needed to schedule an interview with Principal Stinger. But with Dad beaming at me the way he was, I hardly wanted to bring it up now.

At least, that's what I told myself. Deep down, I knew I was avoiding my fear of being sent back to elementary school by keeping my parents in the dark. The interview was going to assess where I belonged, as if I belonged anywhere. My only hope was to hold off the interview until it didn't matter anymore. Until my family left town. Although that wasn't an outcome I looked forward to, either.

. . .

I was tired the next day at school thanks to the long hike on Saturday and the time I'd spent working on the ranch on Sunday. I slogged through until the last period of the day, when my literacy teacher instructed the class to break into groups. She wanted us to discuss a novel that had been assigned as summer reading.

I walked up to her desk as the room dissolved into chaos—kids making eye contact from across the room and sliding chairs into small circles. "Ms. Windle," I said, "I'm new . . . I didn't—"

"Of course! You weren't given the assignment last spring with the rest of the class," Ms. Windle said. "You can just listen in as the others discuss." Then, to my horror, she raised her voice and said, "Class, do any of you have room in your literature circles for one more?"

It was embarrassing. It made it look like I was up there because I was too pathetic to find my own group. Really, I'd only wanted to point out that this was the first I'd heard of the assignment. It was even more humiliating when not a single group volunteered to take me.

At last, Cat reluctantly raised her hand. "Amelia can join us, Ms. Windle," she said, but she didn't sound happy about it.

I did my best to smile as I dragged a chair over to her circle. There were two other girls in Cat's group and one boy. I probably should've known their names, but I didn't.

The four of them shot me obligatory smiles, and then the group broke into discussion.

"I think it would be exciting," Cat said to the others in the group, tolerating my presence, but not going out of her way to loop me in. "Being stranded alone in the wilderness."

"No way," the boy said, "I couldn't handle the food situation." He grimaced. "I need someone else to make sure my dinner isn't moving *long* before I see it, let alone eat it."

I'd read the book after all—a few years back when my family trailered the Gnarly Banana through Canada all the way up to Alaska. Of course, the book had been on Dad's radar. It was about a boy who gets lost somewhere in the North Woods after his plane crashes. All he has is a hatchet his mother gave him, and he must learn how to use it to survive. That was the title of the book—*Hatchet*.

I remembered enough about it to contribute. But I let everyone go on thinking I hadn't read it so I wouldn't have to say anything.

"I saw a bear last spring," a girl with thick bangs said. "Just like Brian did when he found the raspberry bush."

"We've all seen bears, right?" asked the third girl, one with a petite, turned-up nose. "We live in Winterland, remember?" Then she glanced at me and her eyes narrowed. "Except you're new here. So maybe you haven't."

I shook my head. I wasn't lying, though. I hadn't seen *a* bear; I'd seen lots of bears. In Alaska, in Yellowstone, in Washington and Canada. I remembered what David said about his classmates being impressed by his travels. But if I mentioned all the places we'd been, I'd only make a bigger fool of myself.

I was already thinking about how every time my family had spotted a bear, we'd made a joke about it being Beorn from the *The Hobbit*. Beorn was a shape-shifter who could change from a man into bear form. If I got really nervous and another Tolkien reference slipped out—well, I'd seen how well that had gone over with my classmates before.

Thankfully, after I kept my lips locked and shook my head, the conversation passed on. Instead of listening, I let my mind wander. It was the one girl's bangs that did me in. They reminded me so much of Sky's bangs.

The girl with the turned-up nose had an alpaca perma-smile thing going on, too—pert little lips, eternally curled up at the corners. I spent the rest of the period half nodding off and half lost in comparisons while the group droned on about the book.

After school, I hopped off the bus at the stop closest to the Stargazer RV Park. It must've caught Ryan by surprise. He opened his mouth as I passed his row. Apparently, he didn't have an insult at the ready, though. If he ever came up with one, I was too far gone to hear it.

As I approached our campsite, Annie darted out of the woods. Her tail was wagging wildly. I petted her quickly, then popped inside the Gnarly Banana to shed my schoolbag and scarf. When I stepped back out, I snagged Annie's leash from a hook on the trailer.

"Come on, let's go!" I told her. I was hot, sweaty, and winded already from having sprinted from the bus stop. On the positive side, I was wide awake now and my lungs were warmed up for the short jog to Rachel's ranch.

I sensed that the alpacas weren't as bothered by Annie this time as we came blazing down the long dirt drive. After roping her off under the same shady tree, I headed straight for the barn. My breathing was ragged from the run, but I noticed a difference. I was getting used to the high altitude.

Sky greeted me as I walked in. On second thought, *greeted* isn't the word. Greeted implies that I was somehow welcomed. Shunned was more like it. I wasn't spit at this time, but the silver-gray alpaca made it clear I wasn't wanted there. She made a sad and squeaky humming noise and backed away from the fence.

"Don't take it personally," a voice said.

I turned to find Julie smiling warmly and holding a bucket. "She has trust issues. It'll take time, but she'll come around."

"That's what Rachel said, about not taking it personally, right after Sky slimed me."

Julie giggled. She had a pleasant, tinkling sort of laugh. "I heard," she said. "I also heard you got saddled with poop-scoop duty on Sunday. Heath thanks you for that."

"Did someone say my name?" A man stepped into the barn behind Julie. I knew at once he was Rachel's son—he had the same compact frame; broad face; and watchful, wide-set eyes. Unlike Julie, whose feet were clad in the galoshes I'd borrowed last time I'd visited the ranch, he was wearing flip-flops.

"Amelia, meet my husband, Heath. Heath, this is Amelia—she's the girl who rescued you from shoveling manure."

"My sincerest gratitude," Heath said. "I'd shake your hand, but I'm in the middle of bagging said manure for deliveries now."

"Ew," Julie said. "Not in those shoes again."

"It's not like I'm bagging it with my feet."

"Just . . . stop. And promise me you'll wash between your toes before you climb into bed tonight."

"Yes, dear. And behind my ears."

"What's behind your ears now? Nope." Julie raised one hand like a stop sign. "Never mind. I don't want to know."

Heath planted a kiss on Julie's cheek and left the barn.

"Sorry you had to witness that," Julie said after her husband was gone. "And I'm afraid if you were expecting to see Rachel, she's at the shop today. You're stuck with me."

"As long as I get to see the alpacas while I'm here, I'm happy," I said. Then I realized that might sound rude. "Not that I don't want to see Rachel, or you," I quickly added. "You're both great, too."

Julie beamed as bright as the sun. "Girl, you don't have to explain yourself to me. For years, Heath thought I was dropping by for him. But, between you and me, I fell in love with the alpacas first."

"I heard that!" Heath yelled from somewhere out of sight.

Julie laughed, then shouted back, "Now that you know where you stand, maybe you'll start listening to me about the shoes."

I grinned. Their banter wasn't something I witnessed much of. Not that my family didn't tease one another lovingly. But the same jokes got old when you'd heard them a million times.

It hit me that I might *like* being around new people. New jokes. New ideas. New everything. A nagging voice in the back of my head pointed out that I was around new people my own age every day now. And mostly I felt uncomfortable for not fitting in. I tried to push the thought away, but then Julie said, "So you must go to Winterland Middle School, right? I have nieces and nephews there, and friends' kids, and . . . Well, Winterland is a small town. You're in, what? Eighth grade?"

"Seventh," I said.

"Hmm . . . Let's see . . . then you might know Clarissa?"

I shook my head.

"Rajesh?"

Julie proceeded to tick off a string of unfamiliar names.

I strained my brain trying to remember my classmates, but the only two names I could come up with were Cat and Ryan. I knew that wasn't right—I knew far more alpaca names than I knew names of my peers. "I don't know many other students yet," I said.

Julie's lips were curled upward at the corners, but her eyes were sad. They were sad *for me*. I didn't want to see that, so I looked away. Sky had long since stopped humming nervously, but she lingered on the opposite side of the pen. "I can't stay long," I said to Julie while watching Sky. "I should probably get started on the fence."

Julie didn't answer right away. Then she said, "It's true we're shorthanded, and the fence is in dire need of repair . . . but don't feel like you always have to be working to be welcome here. Sometimes you can just enjoy being on the ranch."

I spun back toward her. "Really?"

She smiled. "Really."

"Thanks," I said, wishing I had more than one short word to convey how grateful I was to have found this place. A way to let her know how desperately I needed the ranch and the alpacas in my life.

"Of course! Is there anything you want to see? Anything you're curious to learn more about before you dive right into grunt labor?"

There was one thing . . . I'd left my scarf back at the trailer. As much as I hated not having it around my neck, it really wasn't proper attire for the heat. And it definitely wasn't suited for jogging. "Will you show me how you knit the scarves?"

Julie's face brightened again, all trace of pity gone. "I would love to!" She guided me outside the barn and toward the house. On the back side of Rachel, Heath, and Julie's home was a room filled with sun. Glass panes made up the ceiling and the walls. If it had been circular instead of square, it would've reminded me a little of the carousel. There was more natural light flooding this one small room than any other building I'd ever been in. And with all the trees and wildlife visible from inside, it hardly felt like we'd left the outdoors.

Julie showed me the spinning wheel first. It looked like something straight out of a fairy tale—wooden spokes, foot pedal, and all.

"Once the alpacas are shorn in the spring, we send some of their fleece off to be processed, and the rest we keep for working on projects here," Julie explained. She showed me tubs of cotton-candy-like fibers. "I wash the raw fibers and pick out any burrs or coarse materials. Then I dye the fleece and use the spinning wheel to turn the fibers into yarn."

Julie gestured toward shelves on one side of the room, where balls and loops of yarn were appealingly stacked by color. *Like a rainbow in a room of light*, I thought to myself. But it sounded too childish to speak aloud.

"And this is my loom," Julie said as she led me to a large table in the opposite corner. The loom was slightly more modern-looking than the spinning wheel. It was made from wooden beams and plastic pieces that resembled long white teeth. The rows of teeth held in place lines of white yarn, all stretched in the same direction. Multicolored yarns were woven through in the opposite direction.

"What are you making?" I asked. The cloth was too large to be a scarf.

"It'll be a rug when it's finished," Julie said. "And this"—Julie grabbed a basket with long knitting needles, and a ball of reddish-purple yarn—"is how I make the scarves like the one you purchased at Fleece on Earth.

"Oh, can I watch you knit?" I blurted. "Please?"

Julie didn't answer but instead picked up the needles and began making small, precise movements with her fingers. She demonstrated something called a "seed stitch" where she made loops around one needle, crossed through with the other, and then reversed the process. Actually, there were more steps than that, but I couldn't seem to keep track of them all. Knitting was really complicated, and I was concentrating so hard I lost track of time.

It wasn't until I heard Annie barking outside that I remembered I had a job to do. If I spent all my time learning to knit, the fence repair would never be completed. "Thank you so much!" I abruptly gushed. "But I'd better get to work."

"I knew I liked you," Julie said. "And I appreciate your work ethic."

Annie was wagging her tail when I checked on her. I patted her head, added more water to her bowl, and then set off for the fence.

Without Rachel's help, replacing the first rail felt nearly impossible. I staggered under the weight of the board as I both lifted and secured it between the posts. But I managed. And the second one was easier. As I worked, I watched Samson frolicking around his mother.

He seemed to be growing more sure of himself by the day. Flying bugs now appeared a greater source of curiosity than fear. And while my first few hammer strikes had sent him bounding into the air, after a while, he hardly flinched.

Watching him while I worked made the time pass quickly, and like before, I lost track of it. Only when the sky began to darken did I realize how late it had gotten. *Oh no*, I really wasn't getting any better at keeping track of things. Flustered and anxious that I wouldn't make it back to the trailer before my parents, I quickly stashed away the tools, and then retrieved Annie. We shaved minutes off our time on the jog home. Unfortunately, not enough.

13

Alpacas are hardy animals who can thrive in locations with both very hot and very cold climates.

The truck was parked next to the Gnarly Banana when I got back. I unclipped Annie and let her roam free. Then I took a deep breath and entered the trailer. I expected my parents to pounce on me for being late the second I stepped through the door. But they were so immersed in a discussion, they didn't even notice my arrival.

"I really think if we pull some of our savings and reinvest wisely, we can generate more passive income and get back on the road quicker," Dad said. "Depending on how much revenue we receive from contributing to the Zhangs' blog, we'll most likely be able to fund the Amundsen Adventures for a few more years. At least until Neil starts college."

Mom appeared to be lost in thought, glancing at her lap as

Dad spoke. "If we don't make our move soon, I'm afraid we might get stuck in a rut here," he said.

I held in my breath and tried to be as unassuming as a mouse as I quietly slid to a seated position just inside the door.

Mom lifted her eyes to meet Dad's gaze. "I don't know . . . sticking around for a few more months might not be a bad idea . . ."

I silently nodded in agreement. A few more months sounded good to me. That wouldn't be enough time for me to meet Sky's cria, but it might be long enough for me to finish the fence repair and for Julie to teach me how to knit.

Dad scrunched his eyebrows together in the middle. He made a "humph" noise. "Explain," he said.

"Well, I think we should stick with our original plan," Mom said. "Stay here until after the holidays. By then we'll not only have climbed a fourteener, but we'll also have had the opportunity, and hopefully the ability, to complete the actual Adventure Jar Challenge—Ski a Black Diamond."

"Why?" Dad asked gruffly. "Is it because of the dog? If the kids don't find a good home for her soon, we can always drop her by a no-kill shelter on the way out of town."

Mom glanced through the window. Her gaze landed on Annie where she'd curled up beneath a tree. "No, I mean, I do want what's best for the dog . . . she's very sweet, and loyal, and

I feel more comfortable knowing Amelia Jean has company when she's out jogging." Mom's eyes flicked to me before settling on Dad. "But that's not the reason I think we should stay."

"Then what is?"

Mom seemed to chew on her words before letting them out. "It's been a long time since either you or I have been skiing. I think we might need some time, not only to teach the kids how to ski, but also to get comfortable ourselves before we take on a black diamond."

"Agreed," Dad said evenly. My spirits buoyed. I skipped right over the fact that they were talking about doing something that terrified me, and focused on the possibility of staying in Winterland awhile longer.

"I've made some connections at the deli," Mom said. "People who can give our family lessons and get us up and running at the ski resort."

"That could be helpful," Dad admitted.

As Mom was talking, I secretly wondered about Cat. If Cat was so amazing on the slopes, maybe she could help us learn. But I quickly dismissed the idea. She'd never agree to it. And even if she did, the thought of my family fawning all over her again while I tumbled down the mountain was agonizing.

"And by the time the lifts open," Mom went on, "we'll have been here long enough to get the local pass rate. I just think it makes more sense, economically speaking, to stay where we're at, at least until the holidays. Hopefully by then, we'll be comfortable on skis. And it'll be an easier, more natural break for the kids. A full semester at school, and then back to learning on the road."

Dad had been absorbed with what Mom was saying until that last part. He hadn't seemed entirely on board, but he was considering her points. When Mom mentioned school, though, a light bulb went on over his head. "Oh! That reminds me, a Ms. Horton from Winterland Middle left a message on my phone today. She wants us to call her back first thing tomorrow morning."

In unison, Mom's and Dad's heads swiveled toward me. "Do you know what she wants, Amelia Jean?" Mom asked.

My heartbeat thundered in my ears. I tried to swallow and couldn't. My mouth had grown instantly dry. "Um . . . uh," I stammered. "There's, uh, something I forgot to give you." I grabbed my backpack from the hook by the door and withdrew Ms. Horton's letters.

"Here," I said, forgoing any further explanation.

Mom read both letters even though they basically said the same thing. Then she stared at me, dumbfounded. "This is important, Amelia Jean. How on earth did you *forget* to give these to us?"

Dad snatched the papers from her hands and read. "It's the ranch, isn't it? I knew it would create problems. Starting school is a big change. You don't need to be starting a job now, too. It's too much."

"No!" I protested, maybe a little too loudly, but I was desperate. I was afraid Dad would make me stop visiting the alpacas if he thought my job was the problem. "It wasn't the ranch. I . . . I just forgot."

Dad leaned forward, bringing his face closer to mine. "I think I'm partly to blame. I probably scared you with all this talk of money. We'll be fine. Amundsens are resourceful, right? And, as your parents, it's our duty to provide for you and your brothers. Not the other way around. You don't need to work. Not yet. Not until you've finished school and seen a little more of the world."

He didn't understand. I'd be devastated if he made me quit. Feeling crushed under the weight of his words, I pleaded with my eyes. "I—" I was going to explain that it wasn't like that. That I enjoyed being around the alpacas and working on the ranch. That the work was hard, but also made me feel appreciated and useful.

Then Mom cut me off before I had the chance. "Oh, honey, did you keep this from us because you're worried about being sent back to elementary school?"

"Yes," I admitted, "and—"

"That's ridiculous." Dad spoke over me, his voice heating up. "Have they seen her test scores? If anything, they should bump her up a grade or two."

"We'll set up the interview and get this straightened out right away." Mom tried to placate Dad. "I think Ms. Horton has something against homeschooling, but once the principal meets Amelia, he'll see that sending her back to sixth grade would be a huge mistake."

"He'd better!" Dad said, still spewing a little steam. "I'm sure Amelia is getting good grades and fitting right in with the other middle schoolers."

I finally managed a difficult swallow. If only that were true. I was thankful Mom had steered the conversation away from my job before Dad insisted I give it up. I only wished I was as confident as my parents were that the interview would go the way they expected.

. . .

When we split back into literature circles at school the next day, I listened carefully and made a point of learning everyone's name. Not only did I *want* to fit in, now that there was a chance we'd be staying for the entire semester, I needed to prove to myself, and to Principal Stinger, that this was where I belonged.

The girl with the upturned nose and pert smile was Mia. The boy was Isiah, and the girl with the thick bangs said her name was Sophie. I learned that Mia had moved to Winterland less than a year ago. Really, she was still a "new girl," too. As far as I could tell, though, she fit in seamlessly. That made me doubt myself. Why did I have to be so terrible at making friends?

Then Mia turned to me and asked, "Did you come from a school in the city, too?"

I froze. I wanted to answer, but I was nervous a Tolkien quote would surface again, or some other nonsense that would reveal me as the awkward misfit that I was.

For some reason, though, my mind shot to Sky. I had trust issues just like her. I was timid around new people. I feared they would respond the way Ryan did—with insults and jeers—when they realized how different I was. Then I thought of Samson and how he was overcoming his fears. The thing was, I wanted to be more like Samson. He wasn't brave, but he didn't let his nerves stop him. I wanted to let go and bound around, even if it meant being startled by a bug now and then.

"Amelia?" Cat said. I could feel the group's eyes on me. Everyone was waiting for an answer. I'd been worried I'd say the wrong thing, but not saying anything was weird, too.

"Uh," I said. My hands trembled where I had them clasped beneath my desk. I wanted to shake my head and then turn into a clam. But that was a form of giving up, wasn't it? Had Rachel been right? Did I have grit? Grit was about not giving up, even when you kept failing. Like sawing another board after you cut the first one too short. And grit mattered more than skills, that's what Rachel had said. I wasn't good at making friends, but I thought maybe, just maybe, I had enough grit to keep trying. I took a deep breath and said, "I've been homeschooled since first grade."

"Oh. So, are you from Winterland, then, or somewhere else?" Mia pried. The rest of the group watched me intently.

"Somewhere else." I gulped.

"Where?" Isiah asked.

I still didn't know how to answer that question. It was the same one I'd bombed the first day of school in Mr. Roybal's class with my "not all those who wander are lost" quote. But I really was tired of feeling lonely all day. New people. New ideas. New jokes. I remembered what a kick I got out of listening to Julie and Heath tease each other. I heard Neil inside my head: *Six Crappy Hours of Our Lives. Six hours a day, five days a week, for how many more months?*

I was reluctant to open up, but the alternative—well, that was a lot of lonely. I wanted to feel like I belonged here. After feeling what I'd felt at the ranch—companionship, even from silly, furry creatures, or make that *especially* from silly, furry creatures—I knew if I could feel even a shimmer of that while I was at school, it was worth it to keep trying. I wanted friends.

"All over," I said breathily. It just came out that way—with a whoosh after having been held in so long. "My family moves around a lot. We live in a travel trailer, and, um, go on a ton of adventures, I guess you could say."

Cat stiffened and anger flickered across her face. "So, you just pick up and leave behind the people who care about you?" There was so much hurt in her eyes, I had to look away. It wasn't fair. I wasn't the one who put it there. Not on purpose anyway. The drawing I sent was meant to be a nice gesture, and it wasn't my fault her letters had been lost in the mail. And even though Aunt Catherine was Dad's sister, it wasn't like I'd ever known my aunt, either. I almost said as much—that Cat had no right to hold her mom's mistakes against me—but I thought that might only widen the gap between us.

Instead, I tried to imagine how Cat must feel. Sure, we'd sent her cards in the mail, but we'd always been too busy traveling to get to know her. I was ashamed to think that when we arrived in Winterland I'd wanted her to be an instant friend because we were family. But friendship took effort and commitment. Granted, I'd failed to make any effort the past five years, but maybe there was no such thing as too late. If Cat was worried about my family leaving, did that mean she didn't want me to go? Maybe it all came down to grit again. Even when a way forward seemed impossible, I had to keep trying.

I held Cat's gaze and said, "Yeah, sometimes we do leave people we care about." I thought of how hard it had been when I moved away from my friends when I was seven. I didn't know if it'd been hard for my aunt to leave Cat or not, but I'd like to think that it had. And I knew Cat would want to think so, too. "But it's not easy to leave people, either. It hurts on both sides." I'm proud to say, I cut myself off there. Before I spiraled into the weeds, talking about how much Bilbo Baggins missed the Shire and the other hobbits when he set off on his unexpected journey.

Cat bristled anyway. "Yeah, maybe, but leaving is a choice. Being left behind isn't."

Before I could tell her that it wasn't always—that it wasn't my decision whether I left or stayed, but that if I did go, I would try harder this time to stay connected—Ms. Windle cleared her throat. As she passed by our circle of chairs, she said, "Please save your personal conversations for after school. Right now, you should be focused on the discussion questions I passed out at the beginning of class."

"Sorry, Ms. Windle," Cat said.

Then Sophie read the first and second discussion questions aloud: "Why do you think Gary Paulsen chose the name *Hatchet* for the title of this book? What does the hatchet symbolize to Brian, the main character of the story?"

Since I actually had read the book, but no one else knew that, it seemed to surprise the group when I answered. "I think it's called *Hatchet* because that's all Brian had. He needed the hatchet to survive, but it meant more to him than that. Even though he was mad at his mom, she was the one who gave it to him, so that made it extra important. He still wanted to feel connected to her somehow." I kept my gaze trained on Cat as I went on. "People make mistakes and sometimes they forget it takes effort, but I think there's something inside us that makes us want to be close to family, no matter what."

After I finished talking, I dropped my gaze and chewed my bottom lip nervously. It took me a moment before I was brave enough to peer up at Cat from under my eyelashes. I knew my answer had sounded cheesy, and my heart felt unguarded—like there was nothing to stop it from beating right out of my chest. But I wanted her to know that it was important to me for the two of us to be connected. That we were family, and that I wanted her to be my friend, too—badly enough to keep trying, even if it was difficult for us both.

My fear rating was a strong five and rising until Cat smiled softly and said, "Yeah, I think you're right," and the rest of the group bobbed their heads in agreement.

Alpacas are herbivores and eat only vegetation.

After school, Cat slid in next to me on the bus. I smiled shyly at her. Her cheeks dimpled as she beamed back at me. Then a rowdy group of students boarded and neither of us said anything while I scanned the faces passing by.

"If you're watching for Ryan," Cat said, "you don't have to worry. He has detention today."

I let out my breath and relaxed myself in the cushy bus seat.

"I'm sorry he's been so mean to you," Cat said, then added a second, "I'm sorry." It felt like she was apologizing for more than just Ryan's bad behavior.

"Why do you hang out with him?" I asked.

"I sort of have to. We're both on the youth ski and snowboard team. He's a jerk, but he's stupid good on skis. Really knows his stuff. It's still preseason, so we meet at the Train Car after school. Skiers and snowboarders from other schools meet up with us there. It's really convenient, and they have the best mini doughnuts in the world."

Cat's white-blonde hair was pulled in a high ponytail, and she was wearing athletic clothing, like she did most days. The fact that she was an athlete meant she fit in better with my immediate family than I did, at least in one way. It was weird—she and I looked nothing alike, but something about her chin reminded me of Dad's. I wondered if it was enough for other people to see a family resemblance.

"So, you ski?" I asked, my mind leaping ahead. Like Mom had said, it'd be nice to have someone I knew help me get comfortable on the slopes before I attempted a black diamond—nice enough that I thought I could overcome my jealousy.

Cat shook her head. "Nope. But I've been snowboarding since I was three."

"Oh." My brothers had mentioned her "serious slope skills." I'd only assumed that she was a skier. "You must be really good," I said, and I tried not to sound disappointed. She wouldn't be able to help me tackle a black diamond, at least not on skis. But that was totally fine. I was content just to have someone my age to talk to.

"Yeah, I guess I'm okay," she said. But I could tell she was being humble. Then she swiveled her body toward mine in the bus seat. She bounced the balls of her feet on the floorboard. "I think Ryan has been teasing you to get to me. So, in a way, it's my fault."

"What?" I asked uncertainly. We were finally getting to know each other and if she was responsible for Ryan's cruelty, I wasn't sure I wanted to know about it.

"That first day, when you said something about being lost . . ."

" 'Not all those who wander are lost'?" My stomach churned. I remember thinking it might've been Cat who had told Ryan about it. The thought of her making fun of me still stung.

"Yeah, that. Some of our friends were laughing about it after class. I told them to shut up and Ryan overheard."

"Wait. You told them to shut up?" I was as stunned as I was relieved.

"Yeah, and the way Ryan looked at me and smirked, it was like he smelled weakness. The club is supposed to vote for a new team captain once the season starts. It's between Ryan and me. I think . . . I think part of the reason he's been putting you down is to get under my skin."

"But why would you do that?" I said, still unbelieving. "I thought you resented me. You said it was too late for us to be friends."

Cat shrugged. "I mean, I usually know exactly what I want and who I want to hang out with. But since you showed up, I don't know . . . I'd given up on ever getting to know you. But, whether I like it or not, we are family. And, seriously, I didn't like it at first, but I still felt an obligation to stick up for you. Then your brothers were so friendly, and now . . ."

"Now what?" I inched forward in my seat. I wanted the two of us to be friends, but a part of me was scared she would pull away again.

"Now . . . I like you, too," she said slowly. "You're . . . you're so much yourself. I'm glad you're here."

I got the feeling that Cat didn't go around saying things she didn't mean, and I soaked in the truth of it. "Thanks," I said. "Me too. And . . . and I know I should've tried harder to reach out to you, but, for what it's worth, I never received the letters you sent."

Bafflement mixed with wonder filled her eyes, and I could tell she believed me. Her lips curled upward, then went straight again as she said, "I really am sorry about Ryan. "After that first time, I thought he'd back off if I acted like I didn't care. But I should've told him to stop."

"I wish you would've," I said honestly.

"Maybe we both can next time?" Cat said.

I smiled at her again. I hoped there wouldn't be a next time, but we both knew there would.

"Now, I'm dying to hear about your adventures," she said. "I've lived here my entire life. I'd really like to visit some other places." She paused briefly, then added, "Even though, well, I don't want to be like my mother. I never want to leave Winterland for good."

"Where would you go?" I asked.

Cat didn't hesitate. "The beach."

I raised my eyebrows, not even caring how thick or dark they were in comparison to Cat's thin, pale brows. "Which one?"

"How many have you been to?"

"Um, I'm not sure. I've lost count."

She cast me an envious look and it felt good to be on the receiving end. "Tell me all about it," she said.

So, I told her about surfing in Southern California, and the rocky beaches along the northern Pacific coast. I told her about the soft white-quartz beaches in Florida and the Outer Banks in North Carolina. Then I told her about my family's trip through Canada and up to Alaska.

"I can't believe you've been to the North Woods," Cat said.

"Uh-huh," I said distractedly as the bus rolled to a stop near the Stargazer RV Park. I felt torn. Part of me wanted to jump off and jog to Rachel's ranch. Cat and I weren't finished talking, though, and I didn't want to end it abruptly. I thought it might make things weird between us again. Plus, Rachel had said she was okay with me showing up when I could. It was only one day . . .

"Please don't tell me you ate turtle eggs." Cat groaned, but it had a playful sound to it. "Like Brian did in *Hatchet*."

"What? No! Never!" I said. Then the bus was chugging forward again and the moment for decision was over.

We talked all the way into town and got off near the Train Car and Carousel of Wonder. I felt a wave of longing. I badly wanted to ride Sugar Plum again. Still, Cat and I were just starting to get along. I didn't want to spoil it by doing something that made me appear babyish. For the most part, I could shake off Ryan's insults. But Cat was different. She mattered far more.

A couple other students stepped off the bus with us, the usual crowd that clung to Ryan's side. I was about to say goodbye and let Cat catch up with her group when she looped her arm through mine. "Since there's no ski and snowboard meeting today, want to grab some mini doughnuts with me—they're seriously good—and then we can ride the carousel?"

It was an offer far too good to pass up, and Cat was right about the doughnuts. We split a half dozen of "the works." They came buried in rich whipped cream, caramel sauce, chocolate, powdered sugar, and sprinkles. They were delicious.

After polishing off the last one, we practically skipped next door to the Carousel of Wonder. I hadn't seen Cat's grandmother since she found out I was related to her granddaughter. I was worried she'd treat me differently now that she knew.

"Catherine Alexandria Winter," Cat's grandma said the moment we walked through the door.

I held my breath, half expecting her to chastise Cat for hanging out with me. Instead, she said, "What is all over your face?"

Cat giggled and licked a spot of chocolaty whipped cream from her upper lip.

"You ordered the works again, didn't you?" Carol said, somehow sounding both teasing and exasperated.

"It was necessary," Cat replied. "Amelia Jean has never had the Train Car's mini doughnuts before."

"Hmm, *I suppose*," Carol said. "Go on in and see Dan."

We raced to the back of the building, where we found Dan propped up by his cane. "Girls!" he said. "Please tell me you've come to ride. You're always so busy with school and that team, Cat. I hardly see you anymore."

Cat planted a kiss on his stubbly cheek. "No team meeting today, and you know we came to ride, Dan. Crank up the Wurlitzer."

I climbed on Sugar Plum's back, and Cat hoisted herself upon the nearby dolphin with the ring of flowers around its neck. The carousel sprang to life and the organ belted out a rollicking tune. We whirled around the room, rising and falling along with the menagerie of animals while Dan danced on the center platform, using his cane as a partner. Carol laughed and cheered as she watched from the vestibule.

If I thought riding the carousel was magical before, it was nothing compared to experiencing it with friends. My heart felt swollen with joy as the music filled my ears, and I grew dizzy from spinning and from feeling so carefree. When the ride was over, Cat and I walked out of the building, arms linked again, our conversation bubbly and light.

I hadn't taken more than two steps when I made eye contact with my father from across the parking lot. He clutched a bag of groceries to his chest. The rest of the world was in motion all around, but it was like someone had hit the pause button just on him.

I smiled. No, that's not right. I was already smiling, but I held my lips curled in an upward position when I met his stare. I waved.

It seemed unnaturally delayed, but he raised a hand in return.

"I-I've got to go," I told Cat, and pointed. "That's my ride, but he wasn't expecting me to be here. He's my dad. So, that makes him your, um, uncle."

Cat's smile faltered. I could tell she was scoping him out,

searching for similarities between him and the mother who'd only ever existed for her in pictures.

"Do you want to meet him?" I asked.

Cat worried her bottom lip. She seemed pensive as she unlocked her arm from mine and absently rubbed her fingers together. At last, she shook her head. "Not yet . . . I mean, I do want to meet him. Just, maybe some other time?"

"Okay," I said. I thought I understood. She'd already put herself out there by opening up to my brothers and then befriending me. She probably wasn't ready to let her guard down for all of us at once, though. She had to do it by degrees. That way, there were fewer of us to lose if we abandoned her again. The idea turned my stomach. I couldn't think about leaving now. Leaving was months away. "See ya at school tomorrow, then?" I said cheerfully.

A smiled bounced back onto her face. "I've got nowhere else to be," Cat said jokingly.

Watching for cars, I darted across the lot. "Dad!" I said when I reached him.

He snapped out of whatever had held him in suspended animation like that. He frowned. "I thought you were going for a jog after school today, and to the ranch."

I shook my head, wondering why he sounded so put out. "I mean, I was, but I didn't. I got doughnuts at the Train Car and rode the carousel with Cat instead."

"Cat?"

"Catherine," I said. "She prefers to go by Cat."

"So that was her, huh? Catherine's daughter." Dad peered around me, trying to get a better look, but she'd already gone back inside the Carousel of Wonder. "I'd like to say hello to my niece. To Cat," he said, trying out her name. "Maybe we can spare a few minutes. Your mom will understand."

"I don't think so," I said reluctantly.

Dad balked. "Why not?"

"Because she said she wanted to meet you, but not today."

Dad exhaled heavily and cast me a weak smile. "Fine. Another time, then." His expression grew stern as he switched gears. "Honey, you can't change your plans like that without letting me or your mother know."

"But—"

"I'm glad you and your cousin are getting to know each other," he said. "And I understand that change is hard. You've been forced through a lot of it lately—we all have. Still, Amelia Jean, now that your mom and I aren't around you all day, you have to learn to communicate what's going on with you and your life outside our family." His voice grew tight. "You can't just be wandering around Winterland doing whatever you want whenever you please."

I dropped my gaze and nodded.

He sighed deeply. "I spoke with Ms. Horton today."

My eyes shot back to his. So that's why he was in such a bad mood. "And?"

"And I explained that we're going through some big life adjustments. I apologized for not getting back to her sooner and scheduled the interview for tomorrow. We'll go after your mom and I get off work."

The mini doughnuts caked in sugar curdled and sank in my belly. I didn't say anything as I climbed in the cab of the truck and Dad slid behind the wheel. Maybe if I ignored what he said, the interview would go away.

"Oh, and I want you to skip jogging to the ranch."

"What?" I felt the blood drain from my face. The interview was bad enough. I'd already missed working at the ranch today. I couldn't miss going two days in a row.

"I'm sorry, Amelia Jean. I can't trust you to keep track of time. You were supposed to be back last night before we got home from work, and you weren't. Don't think I didn't notice. So tomorrow, I want you to go straight to the trailer and wait until your mom and I get there. We can't be late to the interview."

Granted, I had been late the night before. But I knew I could get back in time, if he'd give me another chance to prove myself. "Can't I just—"

"No," Dad said, digging in his heels. "School and family come first. No work tomorrow. End of discussion."

The tense mood in the car didn't go away when we picked up Mom at the deli, but she seemed oblivious to it. She blathered on about the lunch rush and running out of provolone cheese. Meanwhile, I stewed over the impending interview and how it would spoil my afternoon the next day, if not my entire school experience. I couldn't bring myself to regret hanging out with Cat, even if it had meant skipping the ranch. But now that I had an actual friend, the prospect of being sent back to elementary school was even more terrible.

Annie ran up as we pulled in close to the Gnarly Banana. She rubbed against Dad's leg as he stepped out of the cab. She wagged her tail and walked beside Dad as he made his way toward the trailer. Dad ignored her.

She seemed desperate for attention, and I felt guilty for missing our run. With all that was on my mind, there wasn't room for trivial things like remembering we weren't supposed to have given the dog a name. "Come here, Annie," I called.

Dad whirled around. The expression on his face registered shock and something else . . . a feeling of betrayal? Then he shook his head as he proceeded into the trailer.

Oops, I thought as I scratched behind Annie's ears and she stared up at me appreciatively.

Mom, who'd been silent as she witnessed the exchange, said, "Annie, huh? I like it." She gave me a sad smile before following Dad's footsteps into the trailer.

Alpacas are intelligent animals. Some are even trained to compete on obstacle courses where they jump small hurdles and walk over, through, and around objects.

C at and I picked up right where we'd left off the afternoon before. School didn't seem so awful and long when I had someone to sit with, laugh with, and share stories with at lunch, and when my entire literature circle wanted me to talk about wilderness survival because I'd had more experience with the great outdoors than any of them.

When I got overwhelmed with the attention and busted out a Tolkien quote, "I am at home among trees," there was a moment of awkward silence.

Then Cat said, "Cool." And Mia, Isiah, and Sophie broke out grins that were friendly, not mocking.

If it wasn't for the nagging sense of dread that I carried around with me, it would've been a good day—one that even

Ryan couldn't ruin, as hard as he tried. He had an insult ready when I hopped out of my bus seat. There was another ski and snowboard meeting, and Cat and the rest of the team were riding the bus into town. While I made my way forward to get off near the RV park, Ryan said loud enough for everyone to hear, "Hey, Brows, are you going off into the wild to join the other hairy beasts?"

I'm proud to say his insult bounced off my newly minted armor. I barely flinched. As promised, Cat bolted upright, ready to come to my defense. But I motioned for her to sit back down.

"That's funny, Ryan. You don't know how right you are," I replied coolly, and raised my awesome eyebrows at him.

He didn't have a comeback for that, which only made me smile. I wasn't sure where the sudden swell of courage had come from. Scratch that. I knew exactly where it came from. I glanced at Cat, and she beamed at me. It came from having friends.

The day felt like a win. So much so that I was able to finally quell the most worrisome thoughts about the upcoming interview. I thought my grades were decent. And I was finding my groove with the other seventh graders—at least in Ms. Windle's class. With Mom and Dad backing me up, the interview was sure to go without a hitch. In fact, I felt so confident that I had everything back under control that I made a snap decision—if I hurried to the ranch and back, Dad would never have to know.

I had plenty of time until he and Mom would be home. Really, it was silly—a waste of time even—for me not to go to the ranch.

The sun was shining brightly and there was a welcome breeze while Annie and I jogged. As we approached the ranch, I appreciated the way the wild grasses swayed in the gentle wind, and how the alpacas seemed extra peaceful today. Julie appeared to be the only one around. I spotted her in a pasture trimming Ed's toenails as he messily chomped on hay.

I tied Annie to the porch post and went to join her. "Good timing!" she said. "Ed here is oblivious." She placed Ed's two-toed foot back on solid ground. "But would you mind distracting Carl while I clip his nails? He always tries to grab the nail trimmer out of my hands."

Julie showed me how to hold Carl's head and pet his neck while she lifted his feet. Since alpacas have only two toes on each foot, they have a total of eight toenails. So the trimming was quick, and I didn't have to worry much about Carl losing interest in the neck scratching and moving on to something else—like stealing the clippers or chewing on my hair.

I helped her with Benny next, and then Lulu, although neither of them seemed to need much distracting. While Julie trimmed, I told her about riding the carousel with Cat and the mini doughnuts we shared. Julie looked up from what she was doing to smile at me. She didn't say anything, but I knew what she was thinking. She was happy to hear I was making friends.

When she released Lulu's last foot from her grip, she said, "I saved this group for last. They're always the easiest. Some of the others had to be restrained. It's been dry for so long and that makes their toenails harder to clip. We really need some rain."

"Did you have to restrain Sky?" I asked.

"I did. It's not as bad as it sounds, though. I harnessed her and tied her to a post. It's a little more work for me, but none of the alpacas really seem to mind it. And it's important that their nails get trimmed so they don't have any foot problems."

"Is she in the barn still?" I asked.

Julie flashed me another smile and said, "She is. Do you want to return these nail trimmers for me and go see her?"

"Sure. But only for a little while. I have to leave early today, and I want to get some work done on the fence." I took the trimmers from her outstretched hands and made a beeline for the barn. As soon as I'd laid the trimmers on the tool bench, I went to see Sky. She didn't really look pregnant—although I wasn't sure what a pregnant alpaca would look like. Maybe it was hard to tell. Maybe that was why a spit-off had been necessary.

As I approached the gate, she avoided eye contact with me. "Hi, Sky," I said. I undid the latch and slipped inside. She hummed nervously. Her gray fleece appeared extra fluffy and soft. Her long eyelashes easily rivaled Lulu's. I so badly wanted to pet her, but I didn't want her to fear me. I took one step forward, and she took one step back.

"Okay," I said, and halted my approach. "Not yet, but I won't give up on you."

Samson, on the other hand, bounded right up to me without an ounce of fear. I'd have sworn that he'd grown an inch taller already. I petted him through the pen and noted what bad shape this part of the fence was in. I needed to finish the section I was working on first, but these rails would be my next priority.

I managed to replace three rotting boards in the same amount of time it'd taken me to replace one the first day. I might've been able to swap out another three if I hadn't been short on time. I quickly cleaned up after myself, then set off to find Julie to let her know I was leaving.

When I returned to the pastures, she was nowhere in sight. I wandered around, looking for her, until eventually, I found myself at the sunroom. I creaked open the door and stepped inside. "Julie?" I called, my voice carrying deeper inside the house. No answer. I circled the room. She'd made progress on the rug being woven on the loom. The colorful yarns were still organized in an appealing rainbowlike manner. I lightly ran my fingers across them. Then I noticed tubs on a table that hadn't been there before.

The first tub held a pile of multicolored fleece—swirls of red, purple, green, and blue. I couldn't resist plunging both hands into the tub, expecting the soft cloudlike feel of Julie's scarves. Instead, the pile of fibers was *wet*.

I raised my fingers to my face. My fingers were wet. Wet with swirls of red, purple, green, and blue. I gasped just as Julie walked through the door. "Sorry, Amelia, I was on the phone with Heath. He—" Julie stopped talking when she saw my hands. "Oh dear."

I was worried Julie would be mad. "I didn't mean to," I said, "I thought—" I couldn't finish because Julie busted out her silvery laughter. She bent at the middle, her body quaking with amusement.

I stood with my hands dripping over the tub, waiting for her to stop.

"That's not going to come off for a while," she said, wiping tears from her eyes. "It's permanent dye."

My stomach somersaulted. "It won't come off?"

Julie, reading my distress, grew somber in an instant. "I'm sorry, Amelia, I shouldn't have laughed. If you could only see yourself, though—like catching a toddler with her hands in the cookie jar." Julie suppressed another giggle.

I tried to smile while I bit back panic. "Isn't there something that can be done?" I didn't tell her that I wasn't supposed to be here today. Or that I had an important interview in less than an hour and had no idea how well rainbow-colored hands would go over.

"We'll give it a try, okay?" Julie said. She whipped up a mixture of baking soda and water, and I scrubbed my hands vigorously at the kitchen sink. The bright colors faded. They didn't go away. After five minutes of water and soap, water and soap, and me anxiously watching the clock above the stove, I gave up.

I held out until the last possible minute, but it was time. Annie kept the rope between us pulled tight as we ran to the RV park. She helped me maintain a swift pace while my mind was occupied. I'd been wearing a scarf practically nonstop despite the heat. Would gloves be a step too far? Otherwise, I'd have to fess up to making a stupid mistake. One I didn't think would help much when I tried to convince Principal Stinger I was a mature seventh grader.

I remembered my mittens, packed away in the extra storage bin at the front of the trailer, and pushed even harder to get there. The parking space next to the trailer was empty. I cut Annie loose and made a sprint for it.

While I was fumbling with the latch on the bin, I heard the crunch of tires on the gravel road behind me. My blood pulsed at the same time a nervous giggle bubbled in my throat. My dread was rising, but it was tamped down by the humorous thought that I was *literally* about to be caught red-handed.

"Amelia Jean?" Dad asked. "What are you looking for?" He stepped down from the cab and made his way toward me.

Hiding was no use at this point. I held out my colorfully dyed hands. "Mittens," I said sheepishly as Mom caught up to us.

"What on earth happened?" she asked.

"It's a long story," I hedged.

"Try us," Dad said. The lack of emotion in his voice was unnerving.

But I spilled everything anyway. How I'd been certain I had enough time to work at the ranch and get back before they returned. How I'd mistaken the freshly dyed fibers for ones that were already dry. And how I thought mittens might be a good idea for the interview. That maybe I could pass them off as a fashion choice instead of cover for a silly blunder.

As the truth came flowing from my mouth and I felt lighter, I could see it weighing down my father by degrees. Before Winterland, I'd always been completely honest with my parents. Granted, I hadn't had much opportunity in the past five years to keep anything from them. But it wasn't like I'd been harboring a deep dark secret. I might've lived a sheltered life, but I knew there were a ton of worse things I could've done than gone to work without their permission.

My parents were silent for the longest time. Finally, Dad said, "I specifically told you to come straight home after school."

"Technically, I did," I pointed out. "And then I went to the ranch."

"This isn't the time to get smart with me, Amelia Jean." The way Dad said it, like I'd just severed his last nerve, made me cringe. "We'll deal with your disobedience later. Right now, we need to leave, or we'll be late to the interview."

· · ·

It was a toss-up which I was fretting over more—facing Principal Stinger for the interview or facing Dad afterward. My throat was tight, and my arm and leg muscles were tensed to the point of shaking on the ride to Winterland Middle. Then there was the creepy way Mom and Dad were staring out the front window of the truck, not saying anything. The silence did nothing to suppress my dread. In fact, the longer it went on, the more nervous I grew.

Worse than the silent car ride was how quiet the school was when we walked in the front doors. Our footsteps echoed down the hallway. If the principal's office were located any deeper in the building, it would've felt like a death march getting there.

I'd seen Principal Stinger in the halls before but never up close. In some ways, he resembled an orc from Lord of the

Rings—short but broad, with high cheekbones, a baldish head, wrinkly skin, and an angry glint in his eye.

"Please, sit down," he instructed my family, then pointed to the three chairs across from his desk. His office smelled like stale coffee and microwaved leftovers. When we'd settled into the seats—some of us less than others—Principal Stinger began. "Now, I understand, Amelia, that you were homeschooled for five years—from grade two through grade six."

"That's right," Mom piped up.

Principal Stinger shrank his back into his seat with a look that I imagined only school principals (and orcs) could give. "I'd like Amelia to answer for herself," he said.

Mom tried to laugh it off. "Sorry, my mistake."

"'Never laugh at dragons.'" I whispered the Tolkien quote half to myself and half to my parents. They glared at me, then both bobbed their heads in Principal Stinger's direction until I understood that they wanted me to reply to his question. It seemed redundant since Mom had already provided the information he was seeking, but I croaked out, "Yes, sir," anyway.

Principal Stinger took in the sight of my colorful scarf and mittens. I instantly regretted my decision to wear them to the interview. Maybe someone like Cat could've pulled it off as a fashion statement—a choice to stand out from the crowd. I was painfully aware, however, that on me, the out-of-season wear appeared to be a child's attempt at dress-up. Like a toddler smearing lipstick on her face or trying on her mother's high heels.

I slid my mittened hands beneath my legs and sat up straighter.

Principal Stinger cleared his throat. "Let's move on, shall we? The test scores you provided to Ms. Horton are high," he said. "But your grades these past few weeks have been . . . inconsistent. Can you explain why, Amelia? Are you finding certain aspects of the seventh-grade curriculum to be too challenging?"

"No," I said, and I wanted to leave it at that. But I also wanted to stay in seventh grade—now more than ever, since I was starting to get along so well with Cat and a few of the others. So I thought the mature thing to do would be to expand my answer. "The work isn't challenging, but . . . but the schedule is. It . . ."

Mom and Dad both seemed entranced, waiting to hear what I had to say. They leaned closer to me, and I noticed Mom was gripping the chair's armrest extra tight. And that was . . . *unsettling*. I'd always relied on them to know everything about me, about my life. Now that I wasn't under their constant watch, they honestly didn't know how school was going for me—if I was sinking or swimming. Principal Stinger had wanted me to answer for myself because I was the only person who could provide answers about me anymore.

"Yes?" Principal Stinger prompted me to continue. "What about the schedule?"

"It . . ." I wet my lips. "It's just that it takes some getting used to. Keeping track of it all. I run out of time on some assignments, because . . . because I spend too long thinking about a topic or a problem. And sometimes, I guess I forget that I need to do things at certain times or be at a particular place when someone wants me to be there. I never had to do that before."

I snuck a peek at Dad, trying to gauge if he was still angry at me for going to the ranch after school instead of staying at the trailer. But his face was like stone.

Principal Stinger's lips, on the other hand, curled into a smile. I decided he might resemble a wizened wizard more than an orc. Not Gandalf exactly, but along those lines. He nodded. "Ah, thank you, Amelia. That's an astute answer. And the other students? Do you feel like you're fitting in here? Making friends?"

I was thankful then that I'd managed to delay this interview until today. Because now, when I said, "Yes, I do. I am making friends," I didn't have to lie.

Principal Stinger smiled again, and I thought to myself, *This is going really well.* Despite Ms. Horton's wishes, I didn't think I'd be sent back to elementary school.

But then Principal Stinger turned his attention to my parents and said, "Everyone's main objective here should be to place Amelia where she's going to be the most successful. It sounds to me like there's been a few bumps, but that she's adapting to seventh grade both academically and socially. My only concern is that she may not yet be as proficient in personal management as her peers. Middle school requires greater responsibility and organizational skills than elementary school." Principal Stinger bent forward and brought his hands together in front of him. "We want our students to be their own advocates. That's why our first few attempts at communication are always through the student. However, I understand Amelia neglected to pass along important information regarding this meeting."

I didn't like the change in direction this conversation was taking, nor the way my dad was nodding in agreement.

"Amelia might benefit a great deal from repeating sixth grade. It would give her an opportunity to learn the nuances of navigating a more structured environment on her own, but with safety nets still in place. Elementary school allows for better communication between staff and parents. And a classroom teacher would be able to provide more individual support as she learns how to manage her time. Middle school is a big jump up from first grade. I wonder if it wouldn't be better for her to ease back into the school system at the elementary level."

Orc! my mind screamed. *Definitely an orc!*

"I don't know . . ." Mom hemmed. "Granted, Amelia Jean did not pass along Ms. Horton's letters. But, overall, I think she's very responsible for her age."

Dad elevated his eyebrows and tipped his head in the direction of my mittened hands as if to say, *Really? You do?*

Mom silenced his nonverbal cues with an icy stare.

At the same time, Principal Stinger said, "As her parents, do you often find yourselves jumping in to rescue Amelia from tricky situations?"

Mom puffed out her cheeks, then blew a stream of air. "Okay. Yes, all the time, but—"

Principal Stinger cut her off. "You don't have to explain. It's only natural for parents to want to smooth the way for their children. But Amelia needs to learn how to rescue herself. It's part of growing up. Ultimately, it's your decision. But I think you should seriously consider where the best place is for that to happen. It might just be in sixth grade."

I shook my head. *This can't be happening.*

"Absolu—" my dad started, but this time it was my mom who did the cutting off.

She placed her hand on Dad's. "Thank you. We need to give

it some thought," she said in way that made it clear the interview was over. "Shall we?" she said to Dad and me as she rose to her feet.

Principal Stinger stood to shake all our hands and then ushered us out the door. I might've been happy to go if my seventh-grader status wasn't still in jeopardy. Little did I know then that far more than middle school was on the line.

16

Because of their similar genetic makeup, alpacas and llamas can be crossbred. The offspring of a male llama and a female alpaca is called a "huarizo."

I deposited myself at the kitchen table and braced for a lecture. I assumed once we were behind closed doors, Dad would feel free to let loose. What he did was far more upsetting. He blew in like a storm cloud and went straight for the computer.

"Dad?" I asked. He ignored me.

"Mom?" I tried. She shrugged and shook her head.

The only noise that filled the trailer for the next ten minutes was the sound of Dad's fingers angrily clicking and clacking on the keyboard. It was beyond uncomfortable, but I felt trapped in place as I waited there, glued to my seat.

Mom busied herself with chores around the trailer—wiping

the table down with a cloth, then folding a bushel of clean laundry.

No one spoke a single word until Dad spun around and faced us. "We'll climb the fourteener the day after tomorrow," he said. "Saturday, we leave for Wyoming. I've booked a spot at an RV park close to Jackson Hole."

Goose bumps instantly rose on my skin, and blood pounded in my ears. *No. No. No. Please no.* I didn't want to leave Winterland now. Not even if staying meant going back to sixth grade. I didn't want to leave when my life here was just starting to feel ripe with possibility. Before I could say as much, Mom belted out, "What? What about our jobs? What about the kids finishing a semester of school? You didn't think to discuss this with me first?"

"We'll make it work," Dad said quietly.

Mom glared. "We've always tried to teach the kids to face their problems head-on. One bad interview and this is your solution—that we just run away from it?"

"It's not that . . ."

"No? Then what is it? Because, to me, this feels an awful lot like cowardice," Mom fumed. Even-tempered, levelheaded Mom was fired up. I would've been shocked if I wasn't already panicking about Dad's decision. The walls of the Gnarly Banana—which were close together to begin with—seemed to be shrinking in around me.

· 202 ·

"We're not ready," Dad said. "We're not ready to reintegrate like this. Not after all this time. It's too much change too fast. Principal Stinger was right. It's too big of a leap, not just for Amelia; for everyone. For heaven's sake. It's been two weeks, and the kids are hiding things from us already."

"Like what?"

"Like naming the dog when I specifically said not to. And traipsing all over town without telling us where they're going. Do you have any idea where David and Neil are right now?"

Mom looked flustered. "At an after-school club? Hanging out with friends, maybe. I guess I don't know . . ."

"That's what I thought. And our daughter completely disregarded my instructions this afternoon. Instead, she went to a job she had no business taking in the first place and got who knows what all over her hands."

I wanted to protest but was still in too much shock. My time in Winterland had just been drastically cut from a few months to a few short days.

Mom inhaled deeply. Afterward, her shoulders curled slightly inward with defeat.

"Amelia isn't ready for this," Dad said. "Principal Stinger said as much. And we're not ready for this, either. There's got to be a way to ease in slower . . . for all of us. I say we get back on the road . . . see how much we can fund writing for the Zhangs'

· 203 ·

blog. Then we'll start signing the kids up for classes at community centers along the way. Maybe do some courses online that require group participation. But this? Diving headfirst back into society? Clearly, this isn't working."

While Mom mulled over Dad's words, I finally found the nerve to speak. I knew better than to bring up the alpacas, but there was something, *someone* rather, important that Dad was forgetting. "What about Cat?" I said. "We can't leave her now."

Dad's eyes met mine. "Amelia Jean, I'm so glad you've had the opportunity to meet your cousin. But that was all this was ever intended to be—an introduction. I feel awful that my sister hasn't been here for her. But your cousin isn't our responsibility. Hopefully, we can stay in touch, but we can't base our life around her. I'm sorry."

And that's what sent me over the edge. "Right," I said furiously, "because with us, nothing is ever permanent. You make us give up everything!" I said. Then I flew out of the trailer, letting the door slam shut behind me.

I didn't want to be, couldn't stand to be, trapped inside the cramped trailer with my parents a moment longer. But, with nowhere else to go, I found a flat log on the edge of the forest and collapsed on top of it. Annie sidled up to me and nudged her wet nose beneath my arm. I stroked her soft red fur and tried my best not to cry.

That's the way my brothers found us a half hour later when they came strolling up the drive. Neil sat down on one side of me, David on the other. We all stroked Annie's back.

After a spell, David asked gently, "Amelia Jean, is everything okay? What's going on?"

I took a deep breath and broke the news.

I expected Neil, at least, to rejoice. He usually loved this part of the Adventure Jar lifestyle—packing our bags and embarking for a new destination. Maybe he was holding back for my benefit, but all he said was "Okay," flat-like—no excitement, no disappointment. Just "okay."

David was a different story. I sensed he was angry but also sad. A storm raged in his columbine-blue eyes as he lightly ran his fingers through Annie's fur. Annie licked his hand in return. "I don't see why we have to go now," he said.

After that, we remained quiet until Mom stepped out of the trailer, a smile frozen on her face. "It's safe," she joked. "Come on inside. David, I think it's your turn to cook dinner."

And that was that. As much time as we spent together, my family members weren't the best communicators. Typically, we gravitated toward action rather than discussion. From what I could gather, though, Mom and Dad had sorted things out. Dad had apologized for acting rashly, but heartbreakingly, the move was still on. The worst part was that I knew it was all my fault.

I'd let Annie's name slip. I'd disobeyed Dad so I could hang out with a herd of alpacas. And I'd messed up big-time at school—proven I couldn't handle seventh grade any better than I could handle rappelling off a cliff.

Shame, anger, and self-loathing warred inside me for the rest of the evening, but the real victor was fear. Fear kept my tongue tied and my emotions bottled inside. I thought about pleading with Mom and Dad to stay in Winterland a while longer. As many times as I'd been forced to overcome my fears, I couldn't make myself speak up. It was the same as when I'd wanted to visit the ranch instead of hiking. I knew, just like then, that the words would never work their way out. Rachel had been wrong about me. I didn't have grit, at least not when it was important. So, I did the only thing I could—I resigned myself to leaving.

17

Alpacas are typically quiet and docile animals. Without sharp teeth, hooves, horns, or claws, they present very little danger.

hat's the point in going to school, if it's our last day?" Neil asked. David shifted in his seat. My bed had been folded and replaced with the tabletop.

I wrapped a colorful hand around my orange juice glass. I'd scrubbed my fingers and palms two more times before bed and a third time this morning, but my hands were still shockingly rainbow colored—a hard-to-miss reminder that our early departure was my fault. My stomach dropped.

Dad, in a cheery mood now that a move was on the horizon, had woken early. He used his upbeat energy to scramble eggs for breakfast. I didn't feel like eating. "To say goodbye?" I answered Neil's question with what sounded like another.

David met my eyes and offered me a weak smile. He wasn't totally sold on the move, either. I could tell.

"Your dad and I have to turn in our resignations and collect our meager paychecks today." One side of Mom's mouth lifted. "I'm betting there are textbooks that need returning, and you should probably notify your teachers . . . and Ms. Horton," Mom said to me. Then she stared into the depths of her coffee mug before adding, "I'll stop by the attendance office after work today to officially withdraw you. But, yeah, let the staff know, and say goodbye to your friends. It'll be good for you to have closure."

Mom continued examining the contents of her mug. I wondered if she was thinking about when we sold our house, picked up everything, and said goodbye to everyone we'd ever known. It was a long time ago, but I remembered the way she'd quietly cried as we drove out of town. Had that given her closure? Goodbyes were hard no matter which way you spun them.

My mouth felt dry, but I needed to speak. There was something I had to ask. "Does that mean I can stop by the ranch and say goodbye to the alpacas? I also need to tell Rachel that she'll have to find someone else to work for her."

Mom glanced up from her coffee. Her eyes darted to the back of the trailer. After Dad finished cooking breakfast for the family, he'd hopped into the shower. He was singing in his deep, off-key baritone, a sign that he was in a really good mood.

Mom focused her attention back on me with an uncertain eye. "I don't know, Amelia Jean . . . Your dad and I aren't very happy with you." She sighed. "You should've listened to your father when he told you not to visit the ranch yesterday."

I allowed my head to slump forward. "I know," I said.

When I glanced up, though, she was smiling softly. "But, yes, you should tell Rachel and say goodbye to the alpacas, too. Go right after school, okay?" she said. "We'll need to get an early start tomorrow if we're going to summit the fourteener before noon. I want you back to the trailer before your dad and I get here."

I sprang from my seat to give her a hug, nearly sloshing coffee out of her cup. My stomach revolted at the idea of climbing the fourteener, but at least I'd get to do one thing I wanted before then.

Later, at school, I avoided drawing attention to myself when I turned in my books and notified my teachers. I waited until after class to speak with each of them. Still, it was incredibly awkward. My teachers tried to act sad that I was leaving. "So soon?" Mr. Roybal asked. "Such a pity! It's only your third week here."

I nodded politely. It was a pity, one I felt deeply even if he didn't. And when a few teachers eyed my colorful hands curiously, maybe trying to make a connection between the stains and my bewildering news, I felt crushed inside. *Yes, it's my fault*, I thought as I offered as little information as possible. "My family is moving. This is my last day." I sounded robotic.

As for Ms. Horton, she was positively gleeful when I told her I was withdrawing from Winterland Middle. She took notes in my folder with orange, purple, and hot-pink-colored gel pens. "This is the right decision. Homeschooling causes many deficits," she said smugly. "But I'm sure another year in elementary school will make up for what you've missed."

When I told her "I'm not enrolling in elementary school" and that I was going back to being homeschooled on the road, she grew rather cross, snatched up her red gel pen, and scratched out everything she'd just written.

With me putting as much distance as possible between myself and the other students, it was like my first few days of school all over. I pretended not to see Cat when she motioned for me to sit by her at lunch. And I hardly said a word in seventh period. I knew it was wrong, but I didn't say a thing about moving to my literature circle. I couldn't bring myself to tell them.

Cat was talking to someone when I climbed on the bus after school. Her eyes drifted to me and she smiled. My flight response kicked into overdrive—muscles tensing, heart pounding. *Get out of here!* my body seemed to scream.

If I ran, though, I'd be just as bad as her mom. I couldn't do that to her. Even if it was difficult to say goodbye, it had to be done. I felt awful for what my family was going to put her through all over again. But ghosting her would be far worse.

The only way I could get through it was to do it quickly before I lost my nerve, so I blurted, "We're leaving." Then I stared at an oily spot where bubble gum had been removed from the bus floor. "My family. We've got a campsite reserved in Wyoming for, uh, next week."

I glanced up in time to see Cat's face freeze. "What?"

"I'm sorry. Really sorry. I promise I'll write to you," I babbled, then I hurried to the back of the bus and found a seat before I fell to pieces. A minute later, Ryan and a couple of eighth graders ambled by and spilled into the row behind me, the last one.

I didn't know if Ryan had moved on to finding other ways to impress the ski and snowboard team, or if he'd given up on teasing me after his insult fizzled flat the last time. Either way, he acted like he didn't even know I was there.

Ryan and the others were speaking in muffled voices, but it sounded like they were excited about something. I tuned them out and gazed at a mountain peak beyond the windowpane. I was heartsick knowing I wouldn't see Cat again. I didn't even want to think about what she must be feeling.

Then there was the fourteener my family still expected me

to conquer. But there was no way they'd summit by noon, not with me there slowing them down. Thank goodness it wasn't an official Adventure Jar Challenge, because this one was doomed to fail. The best I could hope for was that I wouldn't be struck by lightning or fall and need to be airlifted off the mountain.

At least I'd get to say goodbye to the alpacas, but that wasn't going to be easy, either. I thought about how I'd break the news to Rachel. She'd be disappointed. From the way Cat was plastered forward in her seat, I could tell she was disappointed. I'd disappointed my family time and time again and was bound to do so again on the fourteener. I was one big disappointment.

As I stewed over my many failures and shortcomings, the guys in the row behind me grew louder and rowdier. They seemed to be arguing, fighting over something. "Let me see it." Ryan's voice rose above the others as the bus neared my stop.

I saw the bus driver's eyes flicking between the road and the mirror he used to keep track of the students. No doubt, he was troubled by what he saw happening at the back of the bus. He parked along the side of the road, and as I made my way toward the front exit, he hopped up from his seat and made his way toward the back. Our paths crossed in the middle. The stern look in his eyes said Ryan and his friends were about to be in hot water.

Good, I thought. Ryan deserved every bit of what he had coming.

I glanced in Cat's direction, hoping for, well, I don't know what. Some sort of meaningful exchange between us? One last farewell? But her neck was stiffly turned in the opposite direction.

After I got off, I scanned the windows, hoping she'd pop her head out and wave. But the only window open was at the back, near Ryan and his friends. "I don't have anything. See?" Ryan's voice sounded shrill. I was pretty sure Ryan had pitched any incriminating evidence out the window. I guess it wasn't meant to be the day karma finally caught up with him.

I shook my head sadly and took off jogging. I skipped stopping by the Gnarly Banana on my way to the ranch. My backpack was light now that I'd turned in all my books. The only thing in it was my scarf, which I'd removed after school in anticipation of the run.

Even though it panged my heart not to take Annie, I knew the sooner she got used to being left behind, the better. Plus, I wanted to spend as much time as possible with the alpacas, and I'd promised Mom I'd be home before she and Dad got there.

Since Rachel and Julie split time between Fleece on Earth and the ranch, I didn't know who to expect. I was surprised and delighted to find them both sitting on the front porch when I arrived.

"Hey there!" Julie trilled.

"Amelia Jean!" Rachel said with a smile as bright as the Colorado sky.

All my breath, my hopes, my wishes, felt lodged inside my rib cage. I couldn't remember the last time I'd felt so welcomed by anyone outside my family. I couldn't remember the last time I hadn't felt like an outsider. A sense of belonging was a wonderful feeling, and I didn't know when or if I'd ever find it again.

"Hi," I said, doing my best to return their smiles.

"Glad you're here!" Julie motioned for me to step closer. "I was just telling Mom about your hands."

I slowly flipped my palms over and let Rachel see the purple, blue, and red swirls.

Rachel clicked her tongue playfully. "Well, it's official; you're now a bona fide ranch hand. We'll have to get you your own pair of gloves."

"Don't forget galoshes," Julie added.

I forced another smile, knowing I wouldn't be able to hold it together much longer. The grief for what could've been was threatening to sink me. Dad always said he wanted us to live our "best lives." What if my best life was here in Winterland and I'd never get to live it? My lower lip trembled, and Rachel snatched up one of my colorful hands in her own. "What's wrong, dear?"

I shook back the tears. "Nothing," I said. "I just don't have long to stay today. Can I go see the alpacas?"

Rachel gave my hand a quick squeeze before releasing it. "You don't have to ask," she said sweetly and stood up. "I think I've rested long enough. I'll go with you."

"Forgive me if I keep my butt planted right here," Julie said. "It's plain wrong for it to be this hot and dry. I think Heath offered to work at the shop today just to escape the heat."

"You're probably right. Heath has never cared much for the retail side," Rachel said. "Neither did his father." When her voice broke with emotion, it helped me put my own grief in perspective. At least there was a chance I could come back here someday. Rachel would never have her husband back. At the same time, I felt a wave of guilt for leaving her, too. She'd already lost so much.

As we wandered around the ranch, I tried to work up the courage to tell her my family was hitting the road once more—that I wouldn't be able to finish the fence repair. But the timing never seemed right—not with Benny sidling up for snuggles and Lulu vying for our attention. Then Carl nearly teased my backpack from my shoulder while Rachel pushed a bag of grain into my hands and Ed came trotting up. Ed's mouth tickled my hand as he gathered up grains and spilled more than half of them on the ground.

We went to Samson next. He was as lively and adorable as ever, and I lingered near his pen. He came close to the fence, close enough I could run my fingers through the short tufts of fleece around his neck and torso. He would grow up to be a friendly and handsome alpaca. A drenching sadness came over me knowing I wouldn't be able to watch him sprout up and become as soft and fluffy as the others. When he bounded away to investigate something on the other side of the pen, my heart went with him as though it was being tugged away from my body. I whispered a silent goodbye. It was painful to walk away.

And then we came to Sky. She loomed near the fence, close enough for Rachel to stroke her back, while keeping a wary eye trained on me. It was the nearest she'd come, but it was obvious she still didn't trust me.

"Give her time," Rachel said. "She'll come around. You'll see."

This seemed like my opening. I parted my lips to tell Rachel I was moving again, but before I could, Julie burst into the barn. "Mom!" she said, panic thickly lacing her voice. "Come quick. The mountain is on fire."

18

Females almost always give birth to a single cria (kree-ah), although twin births occasionally do occur.

As we exited the barn, Julie pointed to where the sky eerily glowed orange and streams of red ran through the trees. I gasped, feeling all at once struck with horror and awe.

"If the wind picks up, it'll carry it here in no time," Rachel said with a forced calmness. Still, her words conveyed urgency. "We have to evacuate the alpacas."

"But the trailer isn't big enough for all of them," Julie said. "Even if it was, we couldn't pull it. Heath took the truck into town today. And what about the house? Oh, Mom, what are we going to do?"

While they discussed options, I stared in disbelief at the fire. It was impossible to judge the exact location when billows of smoke obscured the view. But it didn't appear to be that far away, and it was in the same direction as the Stargazer RV Park.

My heart drummed. A chill ran down my spine. The Gnarly Banana was empty right now, wasn't it? My parents were still at work and my brothers' school let out later than mine. What about Annie? Had she been waiting for me by the trailer? Where was she now?

With my chest tight and the pounding of my heart drowning out everything else, I didn't notice that Rachel was speaking to me until she gently shook me by the arms. "Amelia, you have to snap out of it," she said firmly. "We're in danger. I need you to start rounding up the alpacas."

I could barely hear her. Fire was deadly. Fire consumed everything in its path. I was standing in its path. Every instinct I possessed was telling me to run. Forget Everything And Run.

"I can't," I choked. I wasn't brave enough. I wanted to be the person Rachel thought I was. Someone with grit and determination. Somebody you could count on when your ranch and your beloved animals were at risk. But I wasn't. When things got dicey, I wasn't capable of providing help. I was a liability. "You need someone else." My parents and my brothers—they were the type of people who could Face Everything And Respond. Not me. I was the one who always ran or needed to be rescued.

"Please, Amelia, there isn't time. There is isn't anyone else,"

Rachel said urgently. "The alpacas might not survive if we don't act quickly."

"You don't understand," I tried to explain. "I'll just make things worse."

Rachel looked me hard in the eye. "No, you won't," she said with so much conviction that I almost believed her.

It took everything within me, everything I'd learned about combating my fears, for me to square my shoulders, take a deep steadying breath, and say, "Okay." I wasn't close enough to the Gnarly Banana or Annie to do anything for them. My self-doubt was as thick as the smoke-filled sky. I didn't think I'd be able to help save the ranch, but I couldn't turn my back on Rachel and the alpacas. "Okay," I said again. "I'll try."

"Thank you," Rachel said, clearly relieved. "There's too much hay and wood around here with the barn, pens, and fences. We can't fully evacuate the herd, but we can move them to a safer location. You and Julie grab as many halters as you can find. Start guiding the alpacas down to the lake. The water's low right now and there's nothing to burn on the beach—without a fuel source for the flames, the alpacas will have a better chance at survival there. Hopefully they'll be okay until the firefighters arrive."

Rachel seemed confident at first, but then a flicker of uncertainty appeared in her eyes. "My husband, he had a checklist of what to do in case of a wildfire. God, how I wish he was here right now."

I grabbed one of her hands in mine and Julie grabbed the other. "It's okay. We can do this," I said. Then, word for word, I found myself saying what Dad had told me hundreds of times. "Just stay calm and focus on what you want to accomplish."

Rachel pursed her lips, steeling herself once more. "The Bible says to not be afraid, three hundred and sixty-five times— that's one reminder for every day of the year. You're right," she said, squeezing my hand. "We can."

I squeezed her hand back and then released it. She pressed her fingers to her forehead. "Let's see . . . Heath cleared the branches and cut back vegetation around the house recently. I'll drag out hoses and fill buckets with water to leave for the fire-fighters." She spoke rapidly while laying out the plan. "While you and Julie are moving the alpacas to the lake, I'll gather mementos and close all the windows. I'm going to park the SUV in the garage facing out. When I start honking the horn, you must come quickly," she said, looking me straight in the eyes. "Do you understand? Saving the ranch isn't worth any of our lives."

I swallowed hard, then said, "I promise."

"Me too," said Julie.

I handed my backpack over to Rachel so it wouldn't slow

me down, and then we broke apart. I was a step behind Julie entering the barn. She quickly pulled halters from drawers and rope leaders from hooks. "We can each handle three alpacas at a time," she said. "We have to lure them into the pens first. Our alpacas are well-trained, but most aren't going to let us harness them in the fields, especially with the fire. They're going to be extra skittish."

While I listened to Julie, I noticed the air wafting into the barn was becoming thicker. The smell of smoke that had started off as faint was growing disturbingly stronger.

After unloading half of the halters and leads into my arms, Julie grabbed a bag of grain. "I'll bring the first group to you. You start leading them to the lake. Then I'll start on the next batch. We'll take turns. Got it?"

"Um, sure," I said even though my nerves were fraying and I had a ton of questions. Not the least of which was—how the heck do you halter an alpaca?

We exited the barn and entered the first pasture. The alpacas there were huddled together and humming loudly. I stood back while Julie used the grain to coax an alpaca toward the pen.

Ed broke free from the herd. Once he was corralled and distracted by the treat, Julie effortlessly guided his nose inside the halter and then pulled the strap around the back side of his head before clipping it in place. *He would be the first tempted by food*, I thought as Julie attached the leader beneath Ed's chin and handed it over to me. "Two more and then you go," she said.

The next two—ones I didn't recognize—were harnessed in no time. As I led my group out of the pen and down the winding dirt path that ended at the lake where Rachel and I rested during my first visit to the ranch, I caught a glimpse of the massive cloud of smoke, and the menacing orange glow beneath it. The sight took my breath away. The fire was growing larger and nearer. It was gobbling up trees the same way Ed gobbled up grains—greedily.

I quickened my step and tried to encourage the alpacas to trot instead of walk. They hummed nervously. The tallest one dug in his feet and made a sound I'd never heard from an alpaca before—shrill and warbling. I assumed it was his warning call.

"Shhh," I soothed. "It'll be okay." It felt weird being the one doing the calming again. I'd always been the one in my family who needed to be reassured. Why was that? Because I was the youngest? Because I was a girl? In my heart, I knew those things shouldn't matter. I could be young and brave. I could be a girl and be bold.

The alpaca pulled back on his leader rope, but I held tight. "A little farther," I insisted as I tugged him forward. "We're almost there."

As we broke through the trees, the reflection of the firelit mountainside in the clear blue lake was startling. The ripples in the water made the flames seem alive as they licked the air and incinerated trees.

The ripples also meant the wind was picking up.

"Come on, Amelia Jean, keep going," I said to myself. I hated how pitiful my voice sounded—small and terrified. But I didn't stop. I searched and found a log large enough to tether the alpacas to, and close enough to the water's edge that the alpacas would hopefully be out of harm's way.

I met Julie on the path back to the pen, along with three more alpacas. "The next batch is waiting for you," Julie said. "I think we can get them all, but we need to hurry."

I nodded and darted off through the trees. Lulu, Benny, and Carl were haltered and penned when I returned.

"Come on, guys," I said, and snatched up their leader ropes, thankful that at least three of my friends would soon be closer to the lake and the small amount of security it provided.

Julie and I tag-teamed like that until the last three had been rounded up from the fields. Each time I headed to the lake, I had to combat the unhurried nature of the sweet animals. They were nothing like Annie, who longed to run when I had her on a leash. Her enthusiastic face popped into my mind and squeezed my heart. Where was she? I pushed the image out of my head.

I couldn't stop to think about her now. Nor could I pay attention to the darkening sky and the fear gnawing at me. I focused only on tugging the alpacas along and delivering them to safety.

While I was bringing the last three pastured alpacas to the lake, Julie said she'd retrieve the ones penned near the barn. I met her on the path on my way back. She was leading Hazel. Hazel's large black eyes were wide and flooded with panic. The sound she made was more like a whimper than a hum. If Hazel's distress wasn't blatant enough, one glimpse at Julie's face told me something was horribly wrong.

I stopped dead in my tracks. "Where's Samson?" I asked.

Julie bit her lip. "One of the rails on his pen is down. He squeezed through. I can't find him anywhere."

A fresh jolt of dread and fear shot through me. I took off running.

"Amelia, wait!" Julie called after me, but I was already gone.

I sprinted, my legs jarring on the uneven trail. I took a short-cut and bolted over rocks, through trees, and around the house and barn to get to Samson's pen. Sure enough, one of the weathered rails was splintered in two. I feverishly scanned the area as far as I could see, but there was no sign of the cria. I was devastated. My chest felt like concrete. My lower lip quivered. I knew it. I knew I would only cause trouble. Samson had escaped, and it was my fault. I hadn't gotten to this part of the fence yet, because

I'd gone to the carousel with Cat and left early for the interview. Dad said I wasn't ready for a job, that I couldn't handle one, and he'd been right.

The harsh air made my eyes sting. My vision blurred. I was worthless. On adventures, at school, everywhere I went, I screwed up. My body felt weighted to the ground with guilt. It was my fault Samson was missing. He was so small and new, and unaware of all the dangers in the world. He was lost, and too little to outrun a fire. He would never survive. I had to find him or I'd never in a million years forgive myself.

Frantically, I scoured the area, darting this way and that. I searched in and around the nearby structures, and under tarps and tree branches—anywhere and everywhere I thought a baby alpaca might hide. All the while, his mother's horror-stricken eyes haunted my mind.

Then, at last, I heard a soft, shrill cry coming from the forest beyond the ranch. I didn't pause to think. If I had, I might've talked myself out of it. As it was, I took off in the direction of the noise. I took off in the direction of the fire.

As soon as I hit the wooded area, I started coughing. I gagged on the thick, smoky air. Deeper in the trees, the fire crackled. Branches sizzled and snapped, then whooshed as they fell to the ground. Panic surged in. It was even more suffocating than the unclean air. My thoughts turned foggy. My body wanted to freeze in place, waiting for someone to swoop in and save me.

I was alone, though. Far from my parents. Far from my brothers. Under the cover of the thick trees, no one would ever find me here. Not before the fire overcame me, anyway.

I had to save myself.

I told myself I was strong, I was willful. Maybe I did have grit. Breathing as deeply as I could, I thought, *I can save myself. But Samson cannot.*

I found the courage to push on. The forest was dark. Every downed log and rust-colored boulder resembled Samson. The ground cover made it impossible to see where I was stepping. I tripped on a stick and split the skin on my knee wide open. The pain caused tears to spring to my eyes, but I didn't stop.

I searched and searched, praying Samson would make another noise. And then he did.

Rushing toward the sound, I found Samson bedded down behind a cluster of shrubs. He stared up at me with big, trusting eyes and hummed. My chest heaved with relief. He was fine, but he wouldn't be if he stayed here much longer. Neither of us would. In one smooth motion, I gathered him in my arms and fled.

Julie met me on the path leading up from the lake. "Thank God, you found him," she said. "I'll take him to his mother. Go get Sky. She's the last one."

I flew back up the path, across the drive, all the way to Sky's pen. No doubt sensing danger in the thick, hazy air, she was backed into a corner. Her hum was high and sharp, full of worry and fright.

"It's all right, Sky." I spoke in my most soothing voice while grabbing a halter and then opening the gate to her pen. It was all I could do to approach slowly, what with the panic still coursing through my veins. I wasn't sure I could ever vanquish my fears, but I realized now that I could get past them. I didn't have to let fear stop me.

When Sky shrieked in alarm, I halted. "Okay," I said. "You come to me." I dipped my hand into my pocket and fished out a small handful of grain. I held my hand as flat and still as possible—which wasn't very still considering the circumstances. Trying as best I could not to tremble, and not to spook the alpaca further with my own apprehension, I said, "Sky, please, you have to trust me."

She quieted but stayed with her haunches planted in the corner of the pen. Her ears moved back and forth, and then flat as though she was listening.

"I know," I said. "New people make me uncomfortable, too. But . . . but I just want to help."

Sky considered me. She blinked her long dark eyelashes. She took one tiny step forward, and then—

A horn blared.

Sky's ears shot upright. She retreated and, at the same time, started humming nervously again.

No, I thought, *not yet*. I wanted to scream my protest but knew I couldn't. Not with the wary alpaca calculating my every move. I'd promised Rachel I'd come immediately, but I couldn't leave Sky here. She, and the baby growing inside her, would be trapped. The flames would burn the wooden barn to the ground with her inside.

I heard more crackling and sizzling—a chilling reminder of what was headed this way. It sounded as close or closer than it had in the forest.

Rachel laid on the car horn a second time.

I took a deep breath. The thick air clogged my throat and lungs. But I stood my ground. I extended my grain-filled hand once more. "It's now or never," I said calmly.

Slowly, miraculously, Sky inched her way forward. Her lips brushed my hand, tickled my skin, as she worked her mouth over the grain.

"Good girl," I said. After that, she gave in fully. I thought she might jerk back when I eased the halter around her nose and clipped it behind her neck. But she didn't. She knew the routine, and I'd finally gained her confidence.

Rachel was sounding the horn in a constant stream as I

rushed Sky out of the barn. Thick, billowing clouds darkened everything around us, the smoke choking out the sun.

Julie darted from the car to meet me. "Come on," she said. "There's no time to bring Sky to the lake. She'll have to come with us."

A deafening crack sounded nearby as a tree fell, its trunk incinerated by flames. Its branches whacked against the forest and the earth, splintering other trees and kicking up dirt.

I gasped. It was here. The fire was upon us.

"Hurry," Julie wheezed as she ripped the back door of the SUV open and helped me usher Sky inside. Sky spilled awkwardly over the back seat—long legged and long necked as she was—leaving very little room for me. I squeezed in beside her anyway.

Julie ran around the vehicle and hopped in the passenger seat. Rachel hit the gas before her daughter-in-law had finished buckling in. The vehicle went barreling through the haze down the long dirt drive.

Beyond my window, pockets glowed orange as fire consumed the dry sagebrush, the trees, everything in its path. Flames sucked all life out of the branches and spread along the forest floor as we drove.

Sky's ears moved back and forth, but otherwise she sat very still beside me.

"It's worse than I thought," Rachel whispered softly, horror-struck.

As we approached the entrance for the Stargazer RV Park, red-hot embers fell on the road in front of us. The temperature inside the vehicle skyrocketed. Of all the dangerous situations I'd been in, this was by far the worst. I'd participated in countless hair-raising activities, but I'd never been in a situation where the fate of so many was on the line. I silently prayed that none of my family members had returned to the trailer early. That Annie had somehow escaped the inferno. That our carload and all the alpacas would be spared.

We heard a loud snap and a blazing tree fell across the road ahead. Sirens blared in the distance—on the *other* side of the fire. There was no way to reach them through the wall of flames.

"Mom, we have to turn around," Julie said, barely able to keep the hysteria out of her voice.

Rachel hit the brakes and threw the SUV into reverse. Then she spun around in a widened section of the road and sped off. "We'll try Olde River Lane instead," she said.

Julie clenched her jaw, then nodded in agreement. "It'll be rough, but anything is better than this."

Olde River Lane was a windy and unmaintained dirt road, with potholes, washboards, and tons of overgrowth. We bounced and jarred. Tree branches scraped at the window and the paint on Rachel's car. I braced myself with one hand on the door and the other trying to secure Sky in her seat as we twisted and turned down the mountainside and were chased by the angry red blaze.

It was rough, as Julie said—the vehicle jostled the entire way. I bumped my head on the roof more than once, and my legs ached steadying myself. But, before long, it was no longer sweltering inside the vehicle. And the temperature kept dropping until it was back in a comfortable range. I inhaled deeply and noticed the air was lighter. I gulped in one sweet breath after another. As we steadily put distance between us and the orange glow consuming the mountainside, my heartbeat slowed, and I was overcome by relief.

We had outrun the fire.

Alpacas require the companionship of other alpacas.
They will become stressed, sometimes ill, if left alone.
They thrive as part of a herd.

A small crowd had gathered in the heart of Winterland—in the parking area shared by the market, the carousel, and the Train Car. Rachel parked near Fleece on Earth, and as soon as we stepped out of the car, Heath ran to meet us.

He enveloped Rachel and Julie in an ardent hug. I stood on the sidewalk holding Sky's lead like a lifeline. The thing was, it seemed like a lifeline for her, too. She stayed close by my side as I worked my way through the sea of people, searching for my family. The air was fresher in town but still laced with smoke.

"Amelia!" Mom spotted me first and raced to reach me. Dad and my brothers followed close on her heels. They surrounded me, touching me as if to make sure I wasn't an apparition. Like they were afraid I'd disappear right before their eyes.

Dad kissed the top of my head and came up coughing. "You smell like charcoal."

"We were so worried about you," Mom said, swiping soot from my cheek. "Thank God you're okay."

My brothers' curiosity quickly turned from me to my furry companion. Neil reached out to pet her, and David walked around to get a better look. But Sky only sidled closer to me, still wary of strangers. Apparently, she no longer considered me one of them.

"Annie?" David asked, his voice steeped with concern.

"I don't know." Moisture gathered in the corners of my eyes. I felt so raw, so exhausted. "I'm sorry. I went straight to the ranch after school."

We turned our attention to the gray cloud looming over the RV park. From this distance, the streaks of fire running down the mountainside looked like waterfalls painted red. We stayed like that for a long time—huddled together for strength and stunned to silence.

Information trickled in over the course of the evening while we lingered about the parking lot. The local volunteer fire department had taken the lead, but wildland crews from all over the state were streaming in to help. Heavy-duty off-road fire engines roared by, carrying hundreds of gallons of water up the road leading to the fire. Helicopters flew overhead carrying buckets of slurry to dump on the flames. Sky raised her head and hummed each time a vehicle or aircraft passed.

A spokesperson for the fire department informed the crowd that wildland crews were cutting a line around the fire. "Our priority is protecting lives and structures," she said.

I was dying to know where Annie was and what was happening at the ranch. But the next words out of the spokesperson's mouth were, "I'm sorry we cannot provide specific information regarding the status of personal property at this point. We're asking that you please register yourselves on the Red Cross Safe and Well site, and a call center has been set up to report missing people."

Unfortunately, there wasn't a call center for missing animals. After the spokeswoman was done talking, my brothers and I approached her, and then two other officials. But nobody could tell us if the alpacas had been rescued, or if they'd seen a dog as red as a Utah sunrise. All the information we received was general—the firefighters were doing everything they could.

Fire containment was reported in percentages—first 10 percent, then 20, and so on. It was a slow battle, but the firefighters were winning. I tried to focus on the positive—that the fire would be put out eventually—but it was impossible not to obsess and worry.

From time to time, someone would approach me and my family. They came to share news or provide some element of comfort. Cat and her grandmother circulated the crowd with a giant box of mini doughnuts from the Train Car. Cat caught me watching her and offered a quick, sad smile but kept her distance.

Dan passed out blankets. Even though it was hot outside, I draped one across my shoulders. It wasn't until the weight of it stopped my tremors that I realized I'd been shaking.

Kids I recognized from school said hello. Younger children walked up and asked if they could pet Sky. She tolerated their attention.

Everyone sort of drifted around, unmoored. Waiting for news.

We learned from Dad's ex-boss that an evacuation center had been set up in the high school gym for those displaced by the fire. "I thought I'd never have to see that place again," Neil said with a groan.

Before loading up in the truck and heading for the school, my parents walked with me and Sky the short distance to Fleece on Earth. Rachel, Julie, and Heath had opened the doors to their business to let in anyone needing to rest or use the bathroom.

They planned to stay at the shop until it was safe to return to the ranch. I passed Sky's rope over to Julie. "I don't think they'll let me keep her inside the gym."

Julie patted the back of Sky's neck. "She can sleep in the storeroom here. We'll need to reunite her with the others as soon as possible. Alpacas are herd animals. They don't like being alone."

I met Sky's eyes, and I could tell that it was true. As distant and aloof as she'd acted in the past, she needed the company of the other alpacas. "Have you heard anything?" I asked.

"Not yet," Rachel said. "But I reported their location to the fire command." She breathed deeply and straightened her back. "I have faith that they'll be all right." Then she turned to my parents and said, "You have a very brave daughter. There's no way we could've gotten our alpacas to safety without her."

A look of surprise flitted across Dad's face. Then he gave my shoulder a squeeze. "Thanks for bringing her back to us. If she was at the trailer—" His voice broke off. "She could've—" He stopped again. I think it was the most fear I'd ever seen in my father's eyes. "I'm just grateful she's here with us now," he said, his voice thick and husky, as if the only way he could get out the words was by dropping it an octave.

Rachel gave my dad a hug and then my mother. "After this is over, we'd like to have your entire family over for dinner and dessert. You can see the work Amelia has done on the fence."

I smiled as my parents exchanged a baffled look. I hadn't told them about the fence.

Heath chimed in, "Yes, please come. You won't regret it. Dad used to say, there isn't a Winterlander alive who can resist Mom's cherry pie. Three-time blue ribbon winner."

Dad smiled and nodded, but the bemusement and curiosity in his eyes had quickly been replaced by a faraway look. The one he always got when he was thinking about the open road. I knew he didn't want to be rude, but he also never planned on cashing in on Rachel's invitation.

"That would be lovely," Mom said politely.

I eyed her questioningly. It really would be wonderful. Even if Dad disregarded the invitation, was there a chance Mom was open to it? How long would we remain in Winterland? Obviously, we couldn't climb the fourteener the next day—not with our hiking gear somewhere inside the evacuation zone. *If it still existed.* Honestly, I'd been dreading the difficult hike, but I never wanted something this terrible to be the reason it got canceled. Our future seemed more up in the air than ever.

"I almost forgot!" Julie said. "Let me grab Amelia's bag." She retrieved my backpack from behind the counter.

I couldn't have cared less about the pack, but I ripped it open and dug out my scarf. "Thank you!" I gushed before burying my face in its softness, then wrapping it around my neck.

I wanted to stay longer, but we were interrupted by a group of people needing Julie, Heath, and Rachel's assistance.

"Come on," Dad said, and motioned for Mom and me to follow.

Even with the comfort of my scarf, my heart was like a lead ball as we walked back to meet my brothers. As we loaded up in the truck. As we headed off for the high school. With all the uncertainty the fire had caused—one thing was definite. Dad was still set on leaving town as soon as possible. Not only that, with all the chaos and confusion, I hadn't been able to tell Rachel I was leaving. I worried I'd never get another chance.

We slept on cots that night, along with thirty or forty other people. The cots were lined in neat rows up and down the gym. Some people had managed to evacuate their homes with a few of their personal belongings. Those who had them tucked their bags securely beneath their cots.

My family, who'd spent the past five years packing and unpacking, arrived with only the clothes on our backs. "Not even a hatchet," I mumbled under my breath, thinking about Brian's plane crashing in the North Woods and wondering how long Winterland Middle School would be closed because of the fire. Even if everything in Winterland shut down, it wouldn't be long before life here carried on without us.

"What did you say, Amelia?" Mom asked.

"Nothing."

There were muffins from the Winterland Bakery and fresh fruit for breakfast the following morning. We barely spoke as we ate, balancing paper plates on our knees and using the cots we'd slept in as chairs. A sullen mood hung over all of us. We all knew that if it wasn't for the fire, we'd be hiking a fourteener that day. Instead, we were waiting to see if everything we owned had been turned to ash.

It was another twenty-four hours before the mandatory evacuation was lifted and we were given clearance to return to the Stargazer RV Park. Dad was a tightly wound knot of anxiety by then. He'd spent all of Friday pacing the gymnasium floor. He'd made endless phone calls to our bank and insurance agent.

We accepted charity from the citizens of Winterland because we had no other options. Community volunteers gave us food and clothing. But it only added to Dad's sour mood. He didn't like having to depend on others.

I didn't sleep well on the cot. It was uncomfortable, but that wasn't the problem. I couldn't stop thinking about the fire and Annie and the alpacas long enough to fall asleep. Plus, there weren't any shades on the gym windows, so everyone was up at the crack of dawn. I kept yawning while Mom drove our family to the RV park and Dad sat in the passenger seat checking his voice mail.

I didn't know what to expect. Mom explained that the fire had been contained relatively quickly. "Sometimes wildfires force evacuees out of their homes for weeks. Sometimes, they don't have homes to return to," she said, and then fell silent.

Was she trying to prepare us for the worst? Even my brothers were quiet then. We'd heard reports that all the mountain properties in the area had been spared, including Rachel's ranch. Homeowners' mitigation efforts had been successful. The firefighters had dug ditches and sprayed rooftops with water—they'd protected lives and structures.

No one came right out and said it, but I knew the campground would've been considered a lower priority—the same way there was a call center for missing people but not missing pets. I didn't like it, but I guess it made sense.

Luckily, there'd only been two other trailers in the RV park when the fire started. And their owners had been able to haul them out of the area before things got bad.

As we neared the Stargazer RV Park and we could see that everything in the vicinity had been scorched to the ground, my stomach turned sour and my heart seized in my chest.

Beside me, David slowly rotated his neck and began

scanning the charred remains of trees outside the window. Neil and I joined in. Even Dad seemed to be watching, hoping, for a streak of red fur to come bursting through all the loss and destruction.

Even though I knew by then that it had most likely been destroyed, when we pulled up to what remained of the Gnarly Banana, I was crushed. Its loss was hard to accept. We'd been through so much with the trailer, it'd almost become one of us. An honorary Amundsen.

An aching sadness ran through my bones. It was devastating to see that the stickers noting all the national parks we'd visited were melted and unreadable. There was a gaping hole at the back of the trailer, and everything was covered in gray soot. The RV wasn't even yellow anymore.

Dad made a sound, almost like a whimper, and Mom reached across the console to give his hand a squeeze. "At least we still have each other," she said. Her eyes circulated the cab before she added, "Come on. Let's go see if anything is salvageable. Shall we?"

Most of the items in the outside storage bin were destroyed, except for the important paperwork and mementos my parents kept in a fireproof safe. My bag had somehow escaped damage, too. I dug it out from beneath what was left of the kitchen table. Dad found the Amundsen Adventure Jar, miraculously still intact, and cradled it like a newborn. We spent the next hour or so rifling through the ruin, loading what wasn't decimated into the bed of the truck and tying it down.

After all his pacing the day before, Dad had come up with a plan. We'd hit the road as soon as possible. Mom and Dad would use their last paychecks to find a cheap rental at our next destination. Southern Colorado had won out over Wyoming since we'd yet to summit a fourteener. As soon as the insurance money came through, we'd get a new trailer. "Thank goodness our policy covers fire damage," Dad had said after he'd gotten off the phone with our agent.

I knew that once we were traveling again, Mom and Dad would start contributing to the Zhangs' blog. We'd go back to living our "best lives" based on slips drawn from a jar. It would be like Winterland never happened.

Except it had, and I knew I'd never be the same. There'd always be a Winterland-sized hole in my heart. And I doubted any other place on the planet could fill it.

I must've been staring off into space as we prepared to leave, because Mom didn't hop in the driver's seat. Instead she walked to where I was standing near the back wheel of the truck. "Are you okay, honey?" Mom measured me with her full-power parent goggles. "You seem quiet. Not yourself."

"I just wish . . ." I had more wishes than I could put name to at that moment. I glommed on to the one easiest to express. "I just wish we could find Annie."

"Me too," Mom said solemnly.

David slunk up beside us—hands in his pockets and kicking the dirt. While everyone else had been scouring our charred belongings, he'd been combing the surrounding area for the stray dog. His face was red and pinched tight. He seemed on the verge of tears or else punching something.

"She's a smart dog," Mom tried to console us both. "I'm sure she fled to somewhere safe when the fire came through."

David blew a puff of air through his nose and nodded. "I just wish we knew for sure."

Mom slung an arm over each of our shoulders. "There's a lot of wishing going around lately."

The way she said it made me wonder what she wished for— the Gnarly Banana back in usable condition, or something else? Something more. Was it possible the Adventure Jar lifestyle was starting to feel hollow and meaningless to her, too?

"Mom—" I started to say something, maybe even something about staying in Winterland awhile longer—I hadn't really thought it through.

But then Neil shouted, "Hey! I found a letter. It was taped to the front door, but it'd swung open, and I didn't see it until now."

Dad finished loading the truck bed and slammed the

tailgate shut. He was the closest to Neil and reached him first. He pulled the folded piece of paper from his hands and read it loud enough that we all could hear. "'Dear Amundsen family, please stop by the Carousel of Wonder as soon as you read this. We have something for you. Sincerely, Dan.'"

My heart ballooned at the thought of riding Sugar Plum one last time. "Can we go? Please?"

"Who's Dan?" Neil asked.

"Do you think he has Annie?" David asked.

"It's not very clear, is it?" Mom said. "He could mean anything."

"He could be a nutjob," Dad said. "I don't see any point in going."

"But he might have Annie," David protested. "We have to go."

"Even if he does, we can't take her with us," Dad said.

Mom shot daggers at Dad with her eyes. And that settled it.

"Fine. We'll stop," Dad grumbled.

Despite his pessimism, I was cautiously hopeful. After the letdown of losing the Gnarly Banana, I needed something promising to cling to. Dan wouldn't toy with us for no reason, and the Carousel of Wonder was the most magical place I knew. I had to believe something good would come from our visit there.

20

A cria weighs eighteen to twenty pounds at birth.

The parking lot was even fuller than it had been the day of the fire. We had to park the truck on a side street a block away and walk the extra distance.

"I wonder what's going on?" Mom asked.

"This is a bad idea," Dad griped. "Let's talk to this Dan and get out of here."

I led the way, zigzagging through the small crowd, my sights set on the carousel. It was weird, though. People I didn't recognize kept stopping to say hello. It seemed like everyone in Winterland was here, and for some reason, they were watching us.

"Small-town people are extra friendly," Neil commented.

I spotted Heath at a table set up in the center of the

commotion. Julie's handwoven colorful alpaca rug was displayed on a rack. A sign tacked to the front of the table read: RAFFLE TICKETS: $5.

"There must be some sort of festival going on today. Look at all the local vendors," Mom said. I detected a note of longing in her voice.

"Can I—" I wanted to ask if I could drop by Heath's booth, but Dad cut me off.

"No. We don't want to get hung up here. I said we could stop and talk to Dan. That's it."

But I'd only gone a few more steps when Cat swooped in from out of nowhere and grabbed my arm. "Amelia," she said, "did you hear? Ryan and his friends caused the wildfire."

"What?" I asked, dumbfounded.

"On the bus ride, right near where you got off . . . apparently, the bus driver saw Ryan toss something out the window. They questioned him and his friends, and they cracked," Cat said. "It was a vape stick. The battery malfunctioned or something. Anyway, it exploded in the dry grass, and that's what sparked the fire."

Ice ran through my veins. The bus driver wasn't the only one who'd seen Ryan tossing something out the bus window. If I'd only known, I might've been able to prevent the fire. I drew my eyebrows together. "Oh no."

My family gathered around. "That's terrible," Dad said. "All that damage could've been prevented."

I withered beside him. *By me. It could've been prevented by me.*

Cat cast an anxious sidelong glance at my mom and dad while keeping her face turned toward mine. "Are you okay, Amelia?" she asked.

The news about Ryan was so unexpected that I'd momentarily forgotten how unsettled things were between Cat and me and that this was her first time meeting my parents.

"Yeah," I said. "Thanks." I shifted my feet on the ground, not sure how to proceed. So, I blurted, "Sorry I didn't sit next to you on the bus on Thursday."

"I'm sorry we didn't talk before you got off," she said.

We exchanged soft smiles.

"Do you think that, um, you might stay longer now that, you know, your trailer was destroyed?" Cat asked. She sounded mostly solemn, but there was a hint of yearning in her voice that nearly broke my heart.

I shook my head sadly as Dad stepped in. "You must be Catherine's daughter," he said. "It's so nice to finally meet you." Dad moved forward clumsily, as if uncertain if he should hug her or shake her hand.

Cat stretched out her fingers and they shook. Then Mom clasped Cat's hand in her own.

"And I'm so glad we have this opportunity to say goodbye," Dad went on. "Our decision to go was rather sudden, and with all that's happened . . . Well, I'm just sorry we haven't gotten to know you better while we were in town."

"Goodbye?" Cat asked. "So, you are still leaving?" Cat took a step backward. She chewed her bottom lip.

"I'm afraid so," Dad said. "Hitting the road from here. But we'd like to stay in touch. We'll send a letter with our PO Box number as soon as we arrive at our next stop, and who knows, maybe Amelia can get her own cell phone when we're back on our feet. That way the two of you can still talk to each other."

Cat smiled wistfully. I think we were both remembering what had happened the last time she tried to send mail. Talking on the phone, or texting, might work better assuming we had cell service wherever my family was located when she wanted to get in touch. "Yeah, maybe," she said. Then she launched forward, tightly wrapping her arms around me in a quick hug. After releasing me, she shook hands with my brothers, and again with my parents. Next thing I knew, she was gone, having slipped away in the crowd.

"Should we go after her?" Mom asked. "We didn't really have a chance to talk."

"No," Dad said, sounding weary and remorseful. "That

might make things even harder on her. She probably isn't one for saying farewell. Catherine was the same way."

"Or maybe she's just tired of people leaving her," I muttered under my breath.

"That news about the boy and the vape stick was disturbing," Mom said. "I read recently that a teenager in Oregon was ordered to pay thirty-six million dollars for starting a massive wildfire. Whoever this Ryan is, he's going to need a good lawyer." I could see the wheels in Mom's head spinning. But she shook it off and said, "Well, we should probably keep moving."

My heart sank when I saw there was a line out the door for carousel rides. I'd been hoping to convince Dad to let me take one last spin on Sugar Plum. But now? There was no way he'd be willing to wait.

"Excuse me. Excuse me," I repeated as Dad, David, and I snaked our way inside the door. Mom said she and Neil would wait outside. I'm pretty sure a few people clapped Dad on the back on the way in. "Sorry to hear about your travel trailer," a man said.

"Thank you," Dad replied stiffly.

Dan saw us coming and hobbled over to greet us. He beamed as he leaned on his cane and shouted. "Amundsen family! So glad you could make it."

"Um, thank you," Dad said again.

David's eyes scanned the crowded building, and I knew he was searching for Annie.

"I understand you, uh, have something for us?" Dad said. I could tell he was hoping it'd all been a mistake—that there would be nothing to tie us to this man or this town. That whatever it was, it wasn't a dog. Better yet, it wasn't something that even belonged to us. Dad's mind was already out the door, and on its way to our next destination.

"This," Dan said, and waved his hand through the air.

David seemed too confused by his answer to be disappointed it hadn't been Annie.

"This?" Dad asked. And the look on his face said, *Yep, I was right—nutjob.*

"Yes, THIS," Dan said, his eyes twinkling. "This is all for you. The carousel rides. The raffles. The Train Car next door is selling pancakes and coffee—all the proceeds from the day go to you—the Amundsen family."

"Really?" I was equally delighted and astounded. I couldn't believe the people of Winterland cared so much about us.

"I . . . I don't understand," Dad stammered.

"It's what a community does," Dan said. "I understand you lost pretty much everything in the fire. Winterland is coming together to help a family in need."

Dad shook his head. "I'm sorry. We can't accept this."

A spark of annoyance flared inside me. Why would he refuse their kindness and generosity? I thought I knew. It'd be harder for him to live the lifestyle he wanted—free of any commitments—if he felt indebted to the people of Winterland for their hospitality. "Dad," I said, hoping I could reason with him.

"No. There's been a mistake." Dad scoffed. "We aren't part of this community. No." He started to back away from Dan. "Give it to someone else. Someone who lives in Winterland. Not us. We're leaving."

Dan's mouth fell open.

"David, Amelia, let's go," Dad said. Then, without saying another word, he bolted. My brother, with his shoulders slumped low, turned to follow.

I tried to swallow my bitter disappointment while I reached for Dan's hand. "I'm sorry" was all I could think to say.

Dan reached his hand out to me and clasped mine in his. "Your dad's a proud man, but perhaps you can change his mind?"

I took a deep breath, still trying to overcome my annoyance. Why did Dad have to be so stubborn? "I . . . I don't know . . ." I said.

"It might be worth a try," Dan gently suggested. "Don't you think?"

I nodded. At the same time, my irritation reshaped itself

into fear. I knew what I had to do, but I wasn't sure I could. It was worth a try, but I was afraid I'd never be able to get the words out. Then it hit me: I was afraid the same way I had been when Dad rescued me on the rappel, and the hike, and countless times before.

But I was also afraid the same way I had been when I'd started working on the fence, and when Samson was lost in the fire, and when Sky wouldn't come with me. The difference was, on those occasions I'd either saved myself or had been the one doing the saving. It *was* possible. I didn't have to be fearless the way my family was. Courage came in different forms. I could refuse to give up, and that was every bit as brave.

Dad stormed through the crowd of well-wishers so quickly, the rest of us could barely keep up. He was halfway back to the truck before I could get his attention. I took a deep breath. "Dad, stop!" I yelled.

He turned to face me with his brows already furrowed. I'm not sure I'd ever been so nervous. I'd have felt more comfortable staring down a roiling ocean wave, a terrifying descent into a canyon, or even another wildfire. Confronting my father was a fear rating ten, for sure.

"Dad, I don't want to leave," I finally choked out.

"Get in the truck, Amelia Jean," Dad said through clenched teeth.

The rest of my words caught in my throat. Heart pounding, I second-guessed myself. I didn't feel brave. Then I reminded myself that being brave isn't necessarily something you are or you aren't. I could choose to act bravely, no matter how afraid I felt.

It didn't come naturally to me like it did for the rest of my family. But I had managed to choose bravery before. And if I didn't choose it now, I'd regret it for the rest of my life.

"No," I squeaked out. "No. You always say you want us to live our best lives, Dad. My best life isn't always setting off for new places. I like having adventures. At least, I do sometimes . . ." I said. "But maybe we can all find what we're looking for right here. Why can't we pack our bags for adventure, but always have a place to come home to? A place here in Winterland."

Mom, David, and Neil were watching the showdown in silence. Their eyes bounced back and forth from my face to Dad's.

"There's literally nothing left for us here, Amelia," Dad said. He didn't sound angry as much as exasperated. "Everything we have is in that truck. All we have to do is load up and go."

"That's not true. Not for me," I said, thinking of the ranch and Cat and all the people who'd gathered in the heart of Winterland today to show us we belonged here. "I have a fence to repair, and I have . . . friends."

"What about school?" Dad asked. "Is staying worth repeating sixth grade?"

I asked my heart the same question, and the answer was yes. "If I have to," I said. "It's not what I want. And I don't think it's right. I *know* I can handle middle school," I said without a shred of doubt. "But if that's that only way we can stay here then, yes, I'll go back to elementary school." I wasn't so worried about fitting in anymore. I thought I could be comfortable just about anywhere as long as it was in Winterland.

My answer seemed to give Dad pause. It wasn't what he'd been expecting to hear.

I felt emboldened by Dad's hesitation. I turned to David. "What about you?" I asked. I badly wanted to stay, but if I was the only one, I didn't want the rest of my family to give up their dreams just for me. "Do you want to leave?"

Dad shifted his gaze to David, and my brother's eyes shot to the pavement. He breathed waveringly through his nose. David had stood by me so many times, helping me overcome my fears. I didn't want to make him choose sides, but I thought he should have a say in something this important. I knew what his answer would've been before Annie went missing. Now I wasn't sure. "It's okay," I whispered encouragingly. "I just want to know."

David lifted his chin and shook his head. "No. I don't want to leave, either," he said. Then he moved by my side.

Dad gritted his teeth.

"And you two?" Dad asked Mom and Neil.

"Hey, I'm happy wherever," Neil said. "I like traveling, but high school isn't as bad as I thought it would be. And it seems like we've only scratched the surface of fun things to do around here. My only request is for a larger kitchen, wherever we end up."

Mom searched everyone's faces before speaking. "A garden would be nice, too," she said. "And I'm not sure, but I think I might want to start practicing law again. Not corporate, but maybe at a small firm. I think I could help . . . people." Mom was never one to lay down all her cards, but I suspected she was thinking about Ryan's case. And, as meanly as he'd treated me, he still deserved someone who would fight for him. Everyone did.

Dad grabbed his head in his hands. "I can't believe this."

"You always tell me not to run from my fears," I said. "But that's exactly what you're doing, Dad. You're scared of staying in one place because you were so unhappy before. Things might be different here. *Please.* Just give it a shot. For me? For us?"

Dad removed the hands covering his face. He studied me, Mom, and my brothers. He inhaled deeply. He exhaled. Then he said, "Okay."

"Okay?!" I squealed.

"Yes!" David said, then slapped me five.

Mom and Neil smiled.

But Dad. Dad looked defeated and sad. My heart broke a little for him. "You're sure you're okay with this?" I asked.

Dad nodded slowly, then swept us all up in a giant hug. "According to Tolkien, 'The greatest adventure is what lies ahead.' The four of you are my greatest adventure. My future. My best life. My everything. If Winterland is where you want to be, then in Winterland we'll stay." Dad cleared his throat. "And I think we're holding up our welcome party, Amundsens. Come on. Let's go thank everyone."

Dad seemed uncomfortable when he apologized to Dan. His cheeks were pink-tinged, and the hair around his face was matted with sweat. Still, I think he was touched that strangers were willing to do so much to help our family. By the end of the morning, Dad had relaxed some. His smile transformed from strained to genuine to flabbergasted when the locals presented Mom and him with enough money for us to pay first and last month's rent on a house in Winterland. Dan even knew of a vacancy not far from Rachel's ranch—one with a large kitchen and a small garden.

There were so many people—kids from school, Mom and Dad's coworkers, Neil and David's friends from their climbing club—who kept vying for our attention.

Finally, Rachel made her way up to me. "Every last alpaca is happy, healthy, and safe, thanks to you," she said.

"It wasn't just me," I answered, embarrassed by the praise.

"But we couldn't have done it without you," she said. "Julie and I were talking, and we think you should have the honor of naming Sky's cria."

"Really?" I asked.

"You bet."

"I . . . I don't know what to name it," I stammered. *Sugar Plum? Serendipity? Frodo?* My mind flooded with options.

Rachel laughed. "Don't worry, you've still got plenty of time. The baby won't make an appearance for another ten months or so."

How long would we stay? I glanced at my dad, who'd been listening in, and he shrugged. At least he didn't shake his head.

Ten months at least, then? We had time. Here in one spot. Time to spend with friends—furry and non-furry alike. Time to watch the seasons change. It felt like such a gift.

Before I could find Cat and ask if she wanted to ride the carousel with me, Neil came running up with a poster in his hand. "Look! Look! You *have* to see this!"

The poster said FOUND DOG. But it wasn't one of the ones with the awful photo of a blurry red mutt that my brothers and I had placed discreetly around town. The dog in this picture was front and center, and unmistakably Annie. This poster had been hung by someone legitimately trying to locate the owners of a lost dog.

"Can we call the number?" David begged. "Please?"

"Well . . ." Dad hedged. "I mean, what's a home without a dog?"

A home, I thought to myself. My chest expanded with relief and I smiled. It had taken all my courage to convince Dad, but the Amundsen family had finally found a place to call home. A home, *and* a dog.

21

The life expectancy for an alpaca is fifteen to twenty years.

at handed me the hammer. While we got ready to replace the next section of fence, Samson stood by, watching us with his big, dark, and inquisitive eyes. Then he kicked his heels up and sprang away.

"He's so adorable. I can hardly stand it," Cat said.

I chuckled. "I know, right?"

She helped me lift the rail and hold it in position while I nailed it in place.

"Thanks for your help today," I said.

"Are you kidding? Rachel's ranch is awesome. Anytime you need help, just let me know."

I was glad she was here. For more reasons than one. The fence repair needed to be finished before a change in weather prevented it. Plus, I enjoyed having my cousin around. We'd been nearly inseparable since my family decided to stay. In fact, she'd helped convince my parents that I belonged with her in seventh grade.

After they learned from Rachel how seriously I'd taken my job, and about how hard I'd been working on the fence repair, and also how I'd kept it together during the fire and saved Samson and Sky, I think my parents were leaning toward having another meeting with Principal Stinger anyway. "Amelia has grown far more responsible in the past few weeks than the school is giving her credit for," I overheard Dad say to Mom the night we moved into our rental. It was weird having so much space and separation—I had my own room—and I'd crept down the hall because it was dark and I wasn't used to being alone.

"You're right," Mom said. "I don't know if it's necessary for her to go back to sixth grade now. She seems to be managing her life better than some adults I know." I crawled back to bed then and slept peacefully through the night.

Then we invited Cat and her grandmother over for dinner, and Cat told my parents all about our literature circle and how the group enjoyed me telling them about our most harrowing adventures with the great outdoors. That pretty much cinched the deal.

Mom offered to handle things with Ms. Horton for me. But

I wanted to take care of it myself. The look on the attendance secretary's face was priceless when I walked through the front door. And when I announced that I would be staying at Winterland Middle, she spilled her entire jar of multicolored gel pens.

I drew my thoughts back to the present and soaked in everything around me. Cat, Samson, Sky's slightly more swollen belly, the pastures full of other alpacas. Even with the blackened trees and charred grasses on the edge of Rachel's property, it all seemed too good to be true.

It had been over a month since the fire. I'd fully adjusted to the structure and demands of middle school. The air was crisper, the sun was less intense—almost muted somehow—and the days were growing shorter. The mountainside had veins of gold where the aspen leaves were changing color, and patches of ashen gray where the trees had been ravished by flames. Already there was frost on the ground when I walked to the bus stop in the mornings. The first snowfall was right around the corner.

Cat handed me the last new rail. I hefted it in place and hammered it onto the fence. "There. It's done," I said, feeling a swell of pride and accomplishment before asking, "Are you willing to help me on the slopes, too?"

Dad said it was up to me whether I participated in the Ski

a Black Diamond Challenge once the ski resort opened. It surprised me to realize I wanted to. That is, I wanted to at least give skiing or maybe snowboarding a try. I would go easy on myself if it didn't work out, though.

"Of course!" Cat brightened. "You'll love it. There's nothing like zipping down the side of a mountain in winter. It's . . . it's the best!"

I wasn't convinced I'd love it as much as she did. Still, as I listened to Cat enthusiastically recite everything she revered about snowboarding, I thought how amazing it was to live in a world where people could chase their dreams and follow their passions. Where my brothers could climb mountains, and Cat could race down them. Where my dad could plan adventures and my mom could plant a garden. Where Neil could experiment in the kitchen, and David had a sweet dog named Annie.

And me, I had the ranch. There would always be bullies and wildfires and people like Ms. Horton who would want to see me fail. It wasn't a perfect world by any means. And I still had fears to overcome. But, as long as there were alpacas in it, I knew living my best life would always be within reach.

Acknowledgments

Alapca my gratitude onto this page! Or, at least, I'll try. For although my appreciation is bottomless, my ability to express my thanks is not.

To my deeply adored editor, Mallory Kass, you once again deserve so much of the credit. You are a wellspring of inspiration, insight, heart, and humor. It is such an honor and a pleasure to travel this road with you.

Many thanks to Maya Marlette, who manages to make me smile with every email she sends, and to all the other fine people at Scholastic who make it possible for me to share my stories. Special thanks to Mike Heath and Yaffa Jaskoll for creating a cover that is beyond adorable.

Thank you to my agent, Ginger Knowlton, and everyone

else at Curtis Brown, Ltd. I am very lucky to have you!

Thank you to all the alpaca owners I spoke with, particularly those at Stargazer Ranch. I had the most delightful encounters with your sweet, furry animals.

Thank you to my readers, and to all the librarians and educators who work tirelessly to put books into the hands of children.

Thank you to all my lovely friends and relatives for the unwavering support. And to Matt, Ethan, Logan and Lucas—thank you for making me feel like I belong on our adventures even when I slow you down. You give me strength and courage in everything I do.

Above all else, my gratitude to God.

About the Author

Jenny Goebel is the author of *Out of My Shell, Grave Images*, The 39 Clues: *Mission Hurricane*, and *Fortune Falls*. She lives in Denver with her husband and three sons. She can be found online at jennygoebel.com.